Short Stories from Days Gone By

Short Stories from Days Gone By

NOSTALGIC TALES OF SIMPLER TIMES

KATHERINE ANNE DOUGLAS

PROMISE
PRESS
An Imprint of Barbour Publishing

ISBN 1-57748-676-5

Published by Promise Press, an imprint of Barbour Publishing, Inc., P.O. Box 719, Uhrichsville, Ohio 44683, http://www.barbourbooks.com

Member of the
Evangelical Christian
Publishers Association

Printed in the United States of America.

Dedication

This book is dedicated to my father, Kenny Vicary.
Love and laughter were the hallmarks of his life,
and he knew how to tell a good story.
We miss you, Dad.

Contents

Preface

Getting older?

Yeah. Me, too.

We need to remind ourselves, however, that the alternative is not getting younger.

It's getting dead.

Yet there are some good things about getting older. One of them is the accumulation of personal stories to retell or simply rethink. The longer we live, the more stories we have to tell. Some are sad; many are painful. Those are the ones God uses to conform us "to the likeness of his Son,"[1] which is quite a marvelous thing when you think about it. Along the way of our "conformation," however, God also gives us stories that bring smiles or laughter.

That's what this collection of stories is made to do—bring some smiles. The longer we live, the more stories we add to our arsenal of "I remember when. . ." and "Can you top this?" The remembering, the telling, and the sharing of our experiences give us a deeper appreciation of others, of our heritage, and of our loving Creator. "Remember the days of old," we're told. "Consider the generations long past."[2] There's a lot to be learned in looking back.

So go ahead and grab your heating pad. Turn on the light. Get comfy in your favorite chair. Read some real-life stories that have been lived by some real-life people. Then reminisce and recall some of your own favorite stories—and share them with someone. The blessing is doubled!

Katherine Anne Douglas

[1] Romans 8:29 (NIV)
[2] Deuteronomy 32:7 (NIV)

Acknowledgments

Susan Schlabach, Senior Editor at Barbour Publishing, Inc., and Debbie Peterson, who was the editor for this book, deserve much of the credit for the work you hold in your hands. The idea for this book was Susan's; Debbie spent many hours editing the manuscript and working with the author, who is an admitted cyberspace illiterate. Thank you, ladies, for all your suggestions, ideas, help, and hard work.

The author wishes to thank each of you who shared something of your lives with me for this book. These are your stories. Thank you so very much for sharing your marvelous memories with me.

CHAPTER 1

Flour Power

Here it is again: the first Saturday of the month and almost eleven o'clock in the morning.

My niece pulls into the driveway of the home I have lived in for almost forty years. As usual, she is right on time. I reach for my cane with a resigned sigh. How I wish I could exchange it for a pogo stick—just like the one we once bought for the boys when they were young! I'd jump and bounce my way to the store!

I would need a tad bit more energy and a tad less arthritis to do that—being nine or ten years old again would help, too. But decades younger I'm not. I'm a grandmother and even a great-grandmother now.

"Come on, old friend," I mumble to my wooden companion of two years. Together my cane and I meet my niece at the front door.

"Hi, Aunt Gaynell! Ready for our trip to the grocery store? Got your list?" My niece's unruly blond curls

(I think they're blond this month) compete to peek out at me from under her fire engine red ball cap.

"All ready. I want to start baking my Christmas cookies next week, so I need to get sugar and flour in addition to my usual assortment of canned soups and cottage cheese."

The two of us get into her van just as we do every first and third Saturday of the month. We chat about this and that as she drives us to the megastore that carries everything from soup to wing nuts. The perpetual sign with a clean-cut young man on it trying to get us to join the store's "team" greets us as we pass through the automatic door. My niece and I split up for a few minutes. She strides purposefully away to one section; I move more leisurely to the fruits and vegetables. I refuse to use one of those team-provided grocery cart/wheelchair contraptions! Woody and I will make our way around the place just fine with a regular shopping cart.

By the time Helen catches up with me, I've made it all the way to the aisle with pudding, spices, and items for baking.

"You are flying through this place today, lady!" she declares, throwing her few items into my cart. I smile in turn at my niece as I reach for a bag of flour.

"Aunt Gaynell, this brand here is on sale," Helen advises me, glancing at another row filled with bags of flour.

"I know. But I always buy Gold Medal flour. Gold Medal flour and I go way back!"

"Really? Did you and your mom use it in baking when you were growing up?"

"Well, yes, but. . . ," I say. My voice trails off and I smile with the sudden reminiscent flash.

"Tell me," she says, a command in her tone. "I can tell there's a story behind that hesitating 'yes.' "

"There certainly is!"

As we make our way through the last of our piled-high rows of food and fixin's, this is the story I tell her. . . .

"It's not easy being a nine-year-old girl. Especially when you're barely into the twentieth century and there are so many things to do and to remember! The wintertime is particularly problematic. First of all, when you get up for school it's still dark. Central heating is still a few years off and it's cold to boot. You have to be sure you have a good breakfast before you start your day, get your bed made, and get out the door in good time. Most importantly, perhaps, you have to layer up with extra clothing to ward off the chill on the walk to school. It's just one more thing to tax the brain and good intentions of even the most fastidious young lady.

"Many young ladies growing up at this time did not have the benefit of fancy store-bought clothes. Mom was the one who made do for you with whatever was on hand. My mother and I were no exception. It's just the way things were back before the likes of Sam Walton and Fred Meijer had their twenty-four-hour-a-day superstores to meet your every material need. Need a dress? Mom made it. Need a petticoat? (We call them "slips" now.) No problem. Mom made it. She could whip you up the necessary garment faster than anyone today can fight traffic over to the megastore for her immediate clothing needs. That's just the way it was then, and the way it is now.

"The smart girl didn't make a big issue about color, size, fabric, or 'go-withs' in her wardrobe. As a matter of fact, she didn't make a fuss about any of those details. (Don't *even* bring up anything like brand names!) Necessity and availability dictated the outcome of the final product. Like it or lump it, as we used to say. Or get the switch to your better side.

"It was on one of these cold winter days that I had my memorable experience. . .and I wasn't the only one for whom it was memorable. In my haste to make it to school on time, I raced out of the house as soon as I had thrown my coat on. I grabbed what I needed for my day at school and trotted off to join the other kids. Things like school buses were a long ways off yet. My friends and I made our way through the rain, sunshine, or snow on our own power to get to school. I mentally clicked off everything as I ran to school; I was sure I hadn't forgotten anything. Breathlessly arriving in the classroom coat-room (back then they were called cloakrooms), I pulled off my coat, eager to get into class.

"TA-DAAH!

"There it was for all the world—well, others in the coatroom anyway—to see: my petticoat without the dress to cover it. It was not a fancy, lacey, delicate under-garment. It was a practical, keep-you-warm, functional petticoat of the early twentieth century. It *was* a brand name, however. In letters big enough to be seen across the county, my gunny-sack-turned-petticoat announced to anyone with eyes to see: GOLD MEDAL FLOUR.

"Blushing to my toes, I threw my coat back on, raced back home to put on the dress I had forgotten, and flew back to school as fast as my legs could carry me. Even nine-year-old girls can be mortified, no mat-ter that others were likely wearing a similar garment under their dresses. It's a day I have never forgotten.

"It's amazing, is it not, that it was two more genera-tions before young ladies were permitted to wear slacks or jeans to school? You would have thought my incident alone would have hurried things along a bit! Maybe the word didn't get around as much as I had feared. . .or those flour people knew a good advertising gimmick even back then. When it comes to flour, only one brand stands out for me! Somehow it has my name written all over it."

Snickering at my shared memory, we take our place in line at the cashier. I shared a final thought with my niece. She had, after all, given her parents—my brother and his wife—a hard way to go back in the late 1960s. (She had counted herself one among the generation of so-called peace-and-love flower children.)

"It just goes to show you," I say, gently thumping my bag of flour with the handle of Old Woody. "There was f-l-o-u-r power long before there was f-l-o-w-e-r power. And it's lasted a lot longer, too!"

CHAPTER 2
There Are Two Sides. . .

Two towheads, the one eight and the other six years old, scrambled into their two beds. Smaller, younger versions of their blond, blue-eyed mother, they snuggled under their covers. The younger pressed her face sideways onto her pillow, her legs tucked up and under her as her mother pulled the blanket up and over her little form. Her upended bottom was higher than her head under the white, nubby, chenille bedspread. Her mother turned to pull the covers over her oldest daughter, who looked up with eyes that showed they weren't quite ready for sleep.

"Tell us a bedtime story, Mom," she said.

"Yeah!" piped up the equally wide-eyed six-year-old. "Do you know any wabbit stories?"

Betty had to smile. Her middle child could not master those *R*s no matter how much they worked with her on pronunciation! But it was too late for a lesson tonight. Perhaps tomorrow they would work on "wabbit," "wooster," and the color "wed."

"I don't think so, honey," she said, reaching to turn off the ceiling light. A shaft of light from the hallway kept the bedroom in muted light.

"Tell us about when you were growing up, Mom! When Grandma and Grandpa kept you!"

"That's our favowit!" the prone towhead agreed.

"Okay, but this is the only one tonight and then you have to go to sleep."

Betty sat on the edge of her oldest daughter's bed and looked on the two faces ready and eager to hear her story. There was little she knew of it herself, really. Just bits and pieces she had coaxed from her foster parents and, under some duress, from her birth father before he died some years back. But she would tell what she did know and then go back downstairs to finish the ironing.

Through one of those little understood, doubtless God-ordained mysteries, she had met and married a man who grew up in the same small town as her birth family. Whenever she got to wondering about what her brothers and sisters were like as children and teenagers, she would ask her husband. He knew them well as school chums and had been good friends with the one brother she never met during his high school years. It wasn't infrequently that telling the girls their "favowit bedtime stowy" prompted her to ask her husband more about the family she only barely knew.

"I was growing up on the farm when I found out I had been adopted," she began, once again telling the story her two girls so enjoyed hearing.

Betty had a childhood that was not unlike that of many children who grew up in the late 1920s and early 1930s. Her mother was a busy farm wife; her father was a tenant farmer. He didn't own any of the lands he farmed or the houses they lived in, but it was a safe and happy life just the same. She and her siblings helped milk the cows by hand. They also learned how to help with the butchering and preparation of their chickens, a task that Betty, the oldest of the five children, found daunting at best. (Details of this task are unnecessary for those of you who have been there. They are *unwanted* for those of you who have not!)

Radio and newspaper were links to the outside world. School, church, and visits to the small town not far away provided them with any pertinent, close-to-home information desired. Summers were times of calling kitties down from trees; one such rescue netted young Betty a scratch on the lip that remained a scar the rest of her days. Entertainment was made, seldom purchased, and often took place right there where the necessary chores of the day were meted out as well.

On occasion a movie would come to the nearest little town and people for miles around would get into town by whatever means they could. Families would spread out on blankets they had brought to their make-shift theater. The excitement mounted as the movie was projected out-of-doors on a sheet or similar silver screen substitute for all comers to watch. Any treats came not out of an automatic corn popper or an electric melted cheese dispenser, but whatever Mom happened to bring —if she, in her own excitement, remembered to bring anything!

It was the tenuous time between the crashing of Wall Street and the rhythmic, ominous marching of Nazi boots. Not a bad time, really, to grow up on a small, somewhat isolated farm in agrarian America. Electricity had made its appearance—even on northern Ohio farms— although indoor plumbing had not quite arrived to make the bathroom the most important room of the house for teenaged girls.

As content as Betty was growing up on the farm with her four siblings, however, there was one unsettled, indefinable thing that gnawed at the edges of her simple existence. And it seemed to Betty, especially as she continued into her teen years, that she was the only one cognizant of it.

It was Betty herself.

For reasons unknown to her, she always felt strangely out of place in her own family. Why that was, she did not know. It did not lessen as she grew older and in some ways intensified as she allowed herself to reflect on the possible *why*s of her unexplainable discomfort.

She was the only blue-eyed blond in a family of brown-eyed, brown-haired siblings. Unlike her brothers and sister, she had an interest in the arts. Her sister took piano lessons; Betty taught herself how to read music and play the piano. She loved writing, drawing, and singing, none of which particularly appealed to her more pragmatic "sibs." There had been family trips to town when she was sure that she had been singled out by an acquaintance of her father's. These disquieting, raised eyebrows and vague questions puzzled her, but she was usually too engrossed with other activities to catch much more than a dropped word or phrase. Curiously, the questions, which were directed to her father anyway, were either ignored or avoided by him. But when she was thirteen years old, Betty's private questions were answered. And she received the surprise of her life.

One afternoon as she helped her mother clean the attic, Betty fell upon two items that piqued her interest. One was a baby book that contained names and dates of all the children of Cecil and Mildred. Except her. That discovery alone sent a peculiar tingle down her spine. The item alongside the baby album, however, charged the tingle. The tingle became a jolt.

The jolt was in the form of an aged newspaper

clipping, one she has to this day. Pictured was a bright-eyed infant with wispy, light hair. Her engaging smile well fit the caption over the photograph which read, "Baby Wants a Mother." The short article went on to describe how Katherine, the youngest daughter of a wid-ower, needed placement in a loving home. The weary, grieving father was feeling the strain of managing a motherless home of six children. The reporter expressed it this way: "[Her] home is a trifle overcrowded with chil-dren and her daddy wants to give her away. . . . Katherine is just the right baby to brighten some lonesome household." As she studied the photograph and read the "advertisement," Betty reflected on the curious absence of her own name and date of birth from the baby album and this newspaper clipping.

Was *she* the baby in the picture? Was this family she called her family not really hers at all? With all the strength of will she could muster as a nervous thirteen-year-old girl, she went to confront the woman she had always called "Mother." Mildred sat busy at the sewing machine. Without aplomb or accusation, Betty held the clipping up before her mother.

"What does this mean?" she asked quietly.

Mildred gave the newspaper clipping the briefest glance and continued on with her sewing. "What do you think it means?" she asked, her attention back on the sewing needle. Betty hesitated only a moment, took a deep breath, and said the words her heart already believed true.

"I think it means I'm adopted."

Silence.

It was clear her mother wasn't going to confirm or deny the statement, so Betty asked her next question.

"Weren't you ever going to tell me?"

More silence. But Betty resolved to wait until she had an answer.

"When you were older," was the cryptic reply from the woman who remained focused on the project at hand.

Betty wondered, *How much older?* But she kept the thought to herself. Finally, her mother turned to her. Betty was surprised to see indignation in her mother's eyes. But there was another emotion there that Betty did not understand at the time. Fear. A fear of discovery she had harbored for over a decade.

"Those people. . . ," she said, her voice clipped and indignant, "were *foreigners!* We couldn't take you back there." She may have wanted to say more, but she didn't. Perhaps she couldn't. She returned to her sewing, dismissing Betty with those few words. That would be all the explanation she would ever give the young girl standing before her. The topic would not come up again for many years.

Betty's emotions, perhaps not surprisingly, weren't as

tumultuous as one might think.

That explains it! she thought. *That's why I've never felt at home in my own family! This isn't my* real *family!*

That adjective would have probably broken Mildred's heart, had she heard it. But she didn't. For her part, Betty felt more relief than shock. And for the time being at least, the knowledge that she had (apparently) been adopted set to rest more questions than it raised. For the next few years she was content to let things remain as they had always been. After all, this was the only family she had ever known! Besides, her mother's disparaging "those people were foreigners" remark conjured up all sorts of intimidating and frightful apparitions for the imaginative girl.

So Betty Louise, nee Katherine Ann, was content to keep her discovery private for some years to come. After all, she was only a girl. It sounded like her parents had rescued her from some terrible situation! At least *now* she knew why she had always felt like she did. Someday she might investigate her roots. But it would not be today or tomorrow. . .or even next year. But perhaps. . .someday.

"So then you met our other grandma and grandpa, Mom?" Her oldest daughter's question brought Betty back to the present. She looked to her youngest daughter, who was now more asleep than awake, and then back at her eight-year-old, who was clearly still very much awake.

"Not quite then. It was later when I saw a newspaper

that said one of my brothers had been killed in the war. That's really how I got to know my real dad, the grandpa you never met."

"Just think, Mom! *Everybody* wanted you to be their little girl! It must have been like being a princess!" She smiled and then yawned, the first sign that she would soon be asleep too.

"Yes, I suppose it was. Time for you to go to sleep now."

The young mother gave her girls each one final kiss good night before peeking in at their baby brother in the adjacent bedroom. She walked down the stairs to the ironing that waited completion and to her husband who knew her family better than she herself did. She might ask him to fill in some more of the "blanks" of those years she missed growing up with her birth family. Telling her story again had stirred up her own curiosity. She might even give one of her biological sisters a call tonight. Perhaps it was a good time to get some more of her own family history!

Chapter 3

. . . To Every Story

I've thought long and hard about what it must have been like for Dad to give away one of his own kids. He would never talk about it. It wasn't his way. So I've had to construct it from my own memories, which are quite vivid." Blanche, now in her ninth decade of life, thought for a moment before continuing. "The longer I live, it seems the more I recall from my earlier years. I not only can remember it, but it's sharper in my memory than last week's news!" The affirming chuckles and nodding heads around the table attested to the truth of her words. "I remember a lot of that terrible year when Mother died. I was fifteen at the time. Since then I've often thought what must have gone through Dad's mind as he struggled through the mid-1920s as a widower with a house full of children. . . ."

It was the hardest thing he had ever had to do.

Harder than burying his wife, who had just died a few months previously at a mere forty-one years of age. He looked again at his wonderful children: Blanche was fifteen, the two older boys were ten and eight, Rose was five, Tony was just over two, and baby Katherine was eight months old. How could he bring more separation to his already devastated family? But he didn't know what else to do! Blanche was exhausted trying to manage a house full of children when she was still a child herself. He was exhausted, too—emotionally, physically, and mentally.

Coleman knew he looked much older than his forty-four years. He had aged rapidly in the few months since his wife's death. His young, vibrant wife was gone! She died of some vague "heart and goiter problem," one day after Blanche had turned fifteen. He was still reeling from the shock. So was Blanche, who had been thrust into the role of surrogate mother and housekeeper for her three brothers and two sisters. Out of desperation, the middle-aged widower had come up with a plan to ease some of the burden from his shoulders and from his oldest daughter. At least until he could bring some order back into their very *disordered* lives.

"I've purchased train tickets for you and your baby sister," he said in a tired voice to Blanche. The other children were busy with various toys and projects for the moment. "I've packed a bag, complete with diapers, for your little sister. The trip should not take long. I think your aunt Mary will be willing to take care of Katherine for a while." His broken English, punctuated by his Hungarian accent, well fit his broken spirit. He tried to inject his voice with more confidence than he felt. He had no guarantees Mary or Cousin Irene, his late wife's closest relatives here in America, would take in his infant daughter for a time. He only hoped they would. Until they got through this topsy-turvy time, he and Blanche could manage the other children. . .or could they? If not, he might have to place some of them with relatives, too. He shook his head at the thought.

One thing at a time. . . , he told himself.

He turned his attention back to his wide-eyed daughter. Blanche was quite mature for her age; he knew she could take care of her youngest sister for the six-hundred-mile trip. He did think the trip would not take too long. After all, it was 1926; trains moved at impressive speeds these days! They should arrive in good time at their aunt's home. He would have to remember to try and contact Mary about this plan of his. Sometime between his busy hours at the music store he owned, placing Blanche and Katherine on the train, and caring for his children, he would contact her. He would have to be sure and write Mary tomorrow.

The trip from the small town of Rossford in northwest Ohio to Philadelphia, Pennsylvania, was not as brief as

Coloman thought. By the time Blanche and Katherine arrived in Philadelphia, the hour was late. Because of a mix-up in changing trains, the arrival of the two sisters was hours later than scheduled. Assuming Coloman had changed his mind and the girls had not made the trip, Mary left the train station without her expected guests. For her part, after many hours on a train, Blanche found herself with a sobbing, starving, soaking infant for whom she had no more dry—let alone clean—diapers! Blanche was not howling or wet, but she was close to hysteria herself.

"I had no idea where to go! Disposable diapers were unheard of in 1926. We were in this huge city and no one met us at the train station! We were miles and miles from home and there we were! I don't know how, but I did remember my aunt's address. We got into a taxi and soon we were on our aunt's front steps." She stopped and shook her head. "I can't imagine what Aunt Mary thought when she saw these two bedraggled waifs at her door at eleven o'clock at night! For my part, I was never so happy to see a familiar face! You can't imagine how well I slept that night!"

Blanche and Katherine enjoyed the kind ministrations of their aunt for a week, but at the end of that time they were returned to their father, who now found himself back where he started. He decided to find a family to temporarily care for his infant daughter. He wasn't sure how people went about these types of things in his adopted country, so he had an article published in their local newspaper. Two different couples came to meet with him and see the baby who was pictured in the newspaper. When Cecil and Mildred arrived, Big Sister Blanche sat by her father obediently.

"I was there as translator—Father's English was always heavily accented—and as my baby sister's advocate. I didn't like the idea of giving my sister away to complete strangers one bit! My father may have thought this was the only solution, but I thought differently. We could do it somehow! But he had made up his mind. I think he was just plain tired and felt he was out of options. I can only imagine what he was thinking at the time. . . ."

Things here in America were not like they were in his country, he thought. In Hungary, when a family had a need, the extended family jumped in to meet that need. It did not seem to be that way here. People were too busy or too poor or too. . .something to give anything beyond their sympathies! Especially when the extended family members were not close by.

He sighed as he tried to make clear to this eager young woman and her stoic husband the arrangement he desired. He just wanted someone to keep Katherine for several months or for a year or two. He didn't know exactly how much time he would need. It would just be a temporary arrangement. He would pay them to help defray expenses. They seemed to understand and they seemed to be a nice couple; it was clear they very much wanted a child. It would be nice for Katherine to be on a farm with a young woman to care for her properly. And the missus seemed enchanted with Katherine.

Who wouldn't be? he thought to himself. She was a happy, beautiful child. When at last they had reached an agreement, they stood. Coloman handed these people some money and some other articles that constituted Katherine's inherited, well-used layette. Last of all he handed them the youngest of his six treasures in the world: Katherine herself.

"We stood at the window together, watching as these strangers took away my baby sister," Blanche said quietly. "His pat on my shoulder was his way of saying 'It will be all right,' I'm sure. But I only saw it as one more loss in our already once-happy family." She was quiet for a few minutes while her nieces, nephews, and other family members waited for her to continue. "But that wasn't the last time we saw Katherine. At least not yet."

Two weeks later, Coloman was shocked to find the couple at his door with Katherine. He couldn't believe it! This was hard enough the first time! Why were these people back?

"We want to keep her," they said to him after an awkward greeting. "We want to legally adopt her."

"No. Just for a short time," he kept repeating. He was frustrated with his inability to make himself understood to these people. What was hard to understand? He just wanted a temporary arrangement! But how did one say "temporary arrangement" in English?

After a prolonged, frustratingly fractured discussion, the young couple and the Hungarian immigrant realized they were at an impasse. The couple rose to leave. They had fallen in love with the blue-eyed, happy Katherine. They did not want to give her up, but they couldn't keep her either—unless it was for a lifetime. Coloman loved her, too, and neither did he want to give her up for anything but a short hiatus. Unable to reach a compromise, the young couple left Katherine with Coloman. If they couldn't have her permanently, they said, they didn't want her at all. Again Coloman watched them depart. And once again he was back where he started months ago.

"I can only surmise that that was what happened. I wasn't at home at the time. I was just happy to have my sister back, although I knew it meant more work for me again. Dad tried to hire a housekeeper, but we had nothing but bad experiences. When he let one of them go, some of our linens went with her. After a few more weeks, he decided again to look for a foster family. That's when the farmer and his wife came back. Unknown to all of us at the time, it would be the last time they would come for

Katherine." Blanche looked across the table to her younger sister. "And it would be the last time any of us would see her for almost twenty years."

"Mildred has missed young Katherine so much," the farmer said with obvious discomfort. He turned his hat nervously in his work-roughened hands. "We've decided to take her for as long as we can have her, if it's still all right with you."

Her dad saw the hope in the red-rimmed eyes of the young woman. She looked at his little daughter with mother-love. It was clear she loved his daughter; he knew she would treat her as lovingly as if she were her own child. Katherine would not be lost in the shuffle of a busy household without the comfort and guidance of a mother. He nodded his assent. The joyful relief in the eyes of Katherine's temporary mother was not lost to him.

So, once again he stood and watched the young farmer and his teary-eyed, but smiling wife take away his youngest daughter. It was a bittersweet farewell for Coloman. But he was sure this was best for them all. For now. After all, it would only be a temporary separation for Katherine from her true family. *Wouldn't it?*

Almost two years passed. Coloman was ready to get his daughter back.

"Dad told me to write a note to Katherine's temporary family, informing them of his plans to come and get her. Tony was the only one of us children not yet in school, so Dad felt he would be able to incorporate Katherine back into the family and still manage his business. I had quit school long ago to care for the younger children and the household, so I would once again be in charge of my little sister. But we got no response to our note," Blanche said with finality.

"My dad drove to the address we had, but no one was there. He had no idea where they were. He came home without our little sister. I remember some things he did, some of the things he said to me or to others. . . ."

Coloman decided to try and make contact with the Halsteads as he had the first time: by newspaper advertisement. He tried other avenues as well, but each attempt only ended in unanswered silence. The farming couple and his youngest daughter had simply disappeared. He did not—he would not—go to the police! This was a family matter! This was something *he* had arranged and *he* would handle! There was no need to drag the police into this!

But all his attempts to locate his daughter met with dead ends. After months of trying, he resigned himself to not seeing his bright-eyed, happy little girl again. As the years passed and his days were filled with the needs of his other growing children, his music store business, and the daily demands of life, he gave up his search.

"I think," Blanche said to her gathered family

members, "that he doubted he would ever see his daughter again. I can only guess what he thought in that year when he finally gave up hope of getting Katherine back, but I think it plagued him for more years and more often than he let on."

He had not been wise to look into the beseeching eyes of the young farmer's wife. If he had not, perhaps he would not have given his daughter to them. He would not have had anything more to do with these people who could not make up their minds! But he had thought to appease the pain he saw in the woman's face when she looked at Katherine. He had made his decision and allowed them to take his youngest daughter back with them. Now he realized that the look in the woman's eyes for his daughter was more than love. It was almost a hunger. He understood that now. He should have known that they would never willingly return her to him once they had her again in their care!

He had given them his treasure; they had given him nothing in return. Nothing! Nothing to say if she was sick or well, growing and happy, alive or dead. The unanswered questions and the dull ache in his heart remained for many years.

"Dad eventually met and married Julia, who was much like himself. . .an immigrant from Hungary who was widowed with two children still at home. This marriage of convenience helped them both through the difficult years of WWII. That's when our brother was killed in combat. Katherine, who knew herself as Betty, saw the obituary. She was in nursing school at the time and told her roommate that the local boy who had been killed was her brother. And, Betty, you can pick up the story from here," Blanche said, turning to the sister who was more than a dozen years her junior.

All eyes turned to Betty, who had learned a lot in the last half hour. It was obvious that her children, now grown with children of their own, were enjoying this as much as she was!

"My roommate called her mother, who knew my real dad. And then Dad called me." It was her turn to fill Blanche in on some details she did not know. "It was a very emotional, tearful reunion. After the crying and embracing, I found out just how angry Dad was. 'What those people did was wrong!' he said. 'I could make trouble for them!' " Her attempt at a Hungarian accent brought smiles among the gathered relatives. Her sister only nodded in knowing agreement.

"'Shush, shush,' said his wife, Julia," Betty continued. "'That was a long time ago, Coloman. Let it go.' Her words no doubt persuaded him. He never said anything to my parents—my foster parents," she corrected herself. "And eventually I got to meet all my brothers and sisters."

"But it's hard keeping them all straight!" her older sister said, smiling at her over their combined tale.

And it was—especially for Betty's children, who grew up with one set of aunts and uncles on one side of the family and three sets of aunts and uncles on the other. On occasion people have been prompted to ask Betty's oldest daughter, "How can you be named after your mother? You have completely different names!"

Then she can tell the two stories above. For you see, this storyteller was given the same name as the bright-eyed infant in that 1926 newspaper photograph. She is my mother.

CHAPTER 4
Availability
and Adaptability

Harriet breathed a sigh of relief as she settled into a chair while her friend, Candace, parked the car. They had come to the airport to pick up her daughter and son-in-law, who were winging their way back from a visit with friends in Alaska. Why anyone would want to visit someone in Alaska was beyond Harriet's imagining! Even more amazing was that someone would choose to live in that snow-packed wasteland!

"Alaska is not at all how you imagine it, Mother," her daughter had said to her before leaving. Harriet knew when her daughter called her "Mother" she was about to get an earful of unwanted information. She had briskly dismissed her daughter's imminent travel monologue under the pretext of getting them both a cup of herbal tea.

"They will probably be late, Harriet." Candace took a seat next to her, ending her reverie of herbal tea and the Alaskan landscape. "Flights that are displayed as 'ON TIME' should read 'LESS DELAYED' or 'ALMOST CANCELED.' "

Harriet had to laugh at her friend's droll humor. Candace was a seasoned traveler herself and was not intimidated by airports or airplanes. She had offered to drive Harriet, who had never gotten a driver's license, to pick up the kids (who were no longer kids, really). That allowed Harriet's husband a free late afternoon to bang away on his new computer.

"Tomorrow I'll be watching Courtney's boys," Candace said. "Her sitter has a sick child at home herself. Wish Courtney could stay home." Harriet looked at Candace, whose expression had become wistful. "Did your mom work outside the home when you were growing up, Harriet?"

"She had to when the Depression hit," Harriet answered.

"Really." It was a statement. "I wasn't born until after the Depression was over. What do you remember about those days?"

"I remember unique food distribution centers and home-baked bread. . . ."

Harriet grew up as one of nine children. Her father was

a carpenter by trade and they lived in a midsized city in the American Midwest. When the financial setback of all financial setbacks hit in the U.S. in the early 1930s, women did then what they do now: They stepped out of the home and into the company of *paid* laborers. That's what Pauline, Harriet's mother, did. The difference between that time and the time of the recession of the 1970s is the stuff from which memories are made. There was no welfare; there were no food stamps. There was no school lunch program. But there were some things that helped big and small families through those years following the stock market's bleak day in October 1929. Harriet and millions of others experienced some of them.

For many there were occasional trips to the nearest neighborhood firehouse—not to schmooze with the firefighters nor watch them wash and shine their engine. In those days firefighters fought fires and (perhaps) rescued an occasional cat up a tree. (The fact is, however, if a cat is left in a tree long enough, he or she will eventually come down. It didn't take firefighters long to figure that out.) Firefighters did not have 911 calls to keep them running day and night for everything from drug overdoses to traffic accidents (with a fire or two thrown in for good measure), so engine houses were available for other needs. In the 1930s one of those needs was food distribution.

When the truck came in with food staples, Harriet and her siblings didn't know (she still doesn't know) from where they came. They just grabbed their wagon and walked the few miles to the engine house to get some of the bags of food made available to them and their neighbors. Big bags of rice, beans, or potatoes would be the selection. Occasionally there would be a bag of oranges! Either way, it was food that would never end up in a grocer's Dumpster or be thrown out onto a compost pile. It would be eaten. *All* of it.

Harriet's mother knew how to do creative things with what she had, whether the food was grown in her own small garden or obtained from the neighborhood engine house. There were no pop-up toaster pastries or waffles-in-a-box. The drive-thru breakfast of eggs-in-a-muffin, believe it or not, was still three decades or more in the future. Pauline, resourceful mother that she was, would occasionally make all the kids a breakfast special: fried bread. Not quite French toast, but likely the poor family's equivalent. She would make up the bread dough and then fry it in a skillet of lard or bacon grease. The big hunks of fried bread were then smothered with homemade syrup: a combination of sugar, water, and a little vanilla. Voila! A quick, easy breakfast—unless, of course, you had to make the bread dough from scratch. Which Pauline did. Not so easy to make, perhaps, but far more memorable than some Breakfast in a Bag.

When Pauline's husband, Herman, had no carpentry jobs, which happened frequently once the Depression was in high gear, he worked as a chauffeur for a wealthy family. For reasons unknown to Harriet, this particular family had no financial problems at this time. Compared to her family, this other family was rich! From Herman's contact with this couple, Pauline occasionally gleaned jobs to bring home extra money. Sometimes she cleaned house for them; sometimes she baked them homemade bread or cookies—a treat for this family who enjoyed store-bought everything, a mystery for Harriet and the rest of her siblings who had never tasted store-bought bread. I don't think Herman and Pauline's employers were interested in fried bread or any of Herman's homemade root beer, however. That might have been what we now call "pushing the envelope." But they did enjoy that homemade bread and cookies, and Pauline was glad to oblige them for the extra earnings the baking netted her.

There was another benefit to be had from this family of means: hand-me-downs. "Benefit" would not be the first word that came to skinny little Harriet's mind in this regard, but it wasn't skinny little Harriet who was trying to keep hearth and home together with things like fried bread dough and beans from the local engine house. It was her mom. And her mom had neither the time nor means for Harriet's wishful wants in 1931. Availability and adaptability were the only dictates for a child's wardrobe in *her* household!

One day Herman's employer, a big woman, no longer

had need of her dark, heavy winter coat. Might Pauline want it? There was no argument there; Pauline thankfully and eagerly took the coat when it was offered to her. She took it home, made some measurements, and grabbed the scissors. Young Harriet was the reluctant beneficiary of this coat that had buttons roughly the size of her head on it. These weren't colorful or clever buttons such as are purchased at fabric stores today. They weren't delicate, attractive additions to a coat that lacked panache and style without them. These were buttons for a large coat for a LARGE WOMAN. Perhaps they had been soigné for a queen-sized, wealthy woman. But that is not what they were for a skinny eight-year-old. They were ugly buttons. Enormous buttons.

"They were MONSTER buttons!" Harriet said, laughing at the memory. "I was beyond embarrassed! It was humiliating! My mother wanted me to wear this coat? In *public?* To *school?* It was all I could do to push those monster buttons through those monster buttonholes! They looked like embroidered pancakes down the front of me!"

"So what did you do?" Candace asked.

"What could I do? I knew I had to wear that coat no matter what."

"Well, if that was the worst of it—"

"Oh, that wasn't the worst of it or the end of it!" Harriet interrupted. "The end of the Depression was still way off in the future. I had one more wardrobe hurdle to clear!"

In the sixth grade—and thankfully, after Harriet had outgrown the monster button coat—her dad received some "script." These vouchers or paper money could only be used for specified items. In this instance, the item was shoes. Harriet was ecstatic! New shoes! For *her!* She could not remember the last time she had had "new" anything! She went merrily along with her parents to choose a new pair of shoes. Visions of vogue footwear sprinted through her head like so many runners at a present-day Boston Marathon. They walked into the store. She was positively squirming with excitement!

There was only one small problem when they arrived at the distribution center.

They did have shoes. They had shoes in a variety of sizes. But they only had shoes for boys. Black, high-top tennis shoes for boys. Unlike what might happen today given this scenario, Harriet couldn't whine her way out of getting a new pair of *boys'* black, high-top tennies. A size was found that fit and that was the end of it. A depression was on; the rule of availability and adaptability was still the order of the day, especially if you were in the family of a blue-collar worker. Particularly if you were in the family of a blue-collar worker with a wife and nine children to support.

Harriet spent her sixth-grade year dreading standing in line, waiting to go into the school. (That's what they did back then—none of this sauntering in when it good and well pleased you.) Trying to cover up one shoe with the other didn't work either. Those boys' shoes came up over the ankles! Long skirts were passe and slacks for young ladies had yet to make their debut into the halls of American schools. So, there she was: embarrassed as she could be. But come winter, she had dry, protected, warm feet. It wasn't even necessary to line them with cardboard! The soles hadn't taken a beating from previous wearers.

Harriet sighed contentedly. "I guess it takes a lifetime of living to appreciate what we did have. I certainly don't stew now over what we didn't have then."

"I think you're right, Harriet. And I think that is our travelers' aircraft pulling in now."

"Candace—will you look at that?" Harriet had lowered her voice to a loud whisper.

A stylish young lady raced by them, readjusting her shoulder bag, pulling her luggage in tow, and glancing at the digital clock on the wall. Her attire was a plaid skirt, a simple turtleneck that flattered her graceful neck, and a coordinating cashmere jacket. Even her hose were color coordinated. She was pert and pretty and obviously on her way to catch a flight for which she was late. On her more-running-than-walking feet she wore black and white high-top tennis shoes.

Harriet and Candace looked at each other and giggled.

"Do you think her mother bought them with script?" Candace asked, standing to her feet.

"I don't know," Harriet replied with a matching grin. "But there's a coat I wish I still had. I think I would have had an interested buyer!"

Chapter 5

The PK

Preachers' kids have gotten a bad rap through the years. They are lumped together as the worst of the worst or as goody-two-shoes, with none falling between either of the two extremes. If you are not a PK, have you ever wondered what it would be like growing up as one? Does it mean you have an unusual life in many ways? Does it mean you spend hours of your free time playing in the church building? Does it mean you are expected to be there every time the church doors are open? Does it mean that sometimes you have to help with cleaning or maintaining the church building? Does it mean your dad doesn't always get paid in cash like everyone else? Does it mean you move around a lot and have to live in some weird houses?

There's an unequivocal, straightforward answer for all these questions: yes. That's exactly what it means.

Gordon began his life as a PK in Ottawa, Canada.

He had one older sister; the two younger sisters were yet to be born. From the time he could barely walk, Gordon was one of those PKs who found himself in a heap of trouble, either of his own making or as a consequence of his life as a preacher's kid.

Frequently.

Inside the church and outside the church. It would turn out to be the pattern of his life as a child. His parents should have considered themselves forewarned when Gordon was three years old. They were going to have some trying times with this son of theirs. Gordon's dad didn't preach about prayer from some idyllic or utopian summit. From his son's mishaps the preacher would learn much about the power of prayer. He learned it like we all learn it, really: in the trenches of everyday living.

As his dad prepared to enter the ministry, Gordon walked out of infancy into toddlerhood. One day he walked into the kitchen where he was intrigued by a food he had never seen before: fuzzy blue grapes. Ah! After one sampling he knew this fruit was appealing to the flesh as well as to the eye! He ate another and then another. That furry tickle was a unique experience! He'd never had furry food to eat before—not to mention that it was *blue* furry food! No one was around. He continued popping one grape after another into his mouth. As a preschooler, it never occurred to him that these grapes were bound for the garbage. He merrily consumed the whole fuzzy bunch.

Gordon was one very sick and then very sleepy little boy before his mother realized that this wasn't some "bug" her son would shake off in a day or two. She had no idea how he became so ill so quickly. It wasn't long before she was worried—very worried. And then she discovered the missing moldy grapes. She rushed her seriously ill son to the hospital, where he further deteriorated. It was another day or two before her husband was able to race home from Nyack, New York. Gordon was already in a coma. The doctor informed them he was a victim of ptomaine poisoning and that their son's prognosis was not good. After several days, the physician told Gordon's parents, Dick and Della, that their son would not recover. His expression was grave.

"He won't be alive tomorrow morning. He's not going to make it," he said.

"Yes, he is," asserted Dick.

The physician didn't argue with Dick. He knew what he knew and he knew this child was not going to survive the night. Nothing else medically could be done for the three-year-old boy.

Dick and Della went home. The aspiring young preacher called upon everyone in their church to pray by turns for Gordon throughout the night. After their own time of fervent prayer and intercession, this young couple fell into a confidant, restful sleep, trusting God to heal their son. The first words of welcome the pusher of prayer heard when he arrived at the hospital the next morning were "Hi, Daddy!"

Gordon had a steady diet of cream for weeks afterwards. The liquid was to allow his stomach and intestinal tract to heal from the ravages of the poisoning. To this day, surprisingly perhaps, Gordon loves cream. Sometimes he has a little coffee or some fresh berries with it. Not surprisingly, he *cannot* take penicillin. That whopping dose when he was a toddler is all the penicillin his body ever wants to see again! But he was just a toddler, and he was just getting "warmed up." His father, however, became an avid advocate for calling on and depending on the Lord in illness—no matter what or whose the diagnosis.

One of Gordon's first memories concerning the church was when he was five or six years old. His dad had taken a church in northern Maine that was meeting in a hall. Another church in town had burned down and was rebuilding. They donated their charred pews to Dick and his beginning work. Gordon remembers sanding and painting those pews. It was not a task he enjoyed. As they moved from the meeting hall to a real church building, Gordon's interest in church continued to be less than enthusiastic. He was a little boy, after all. Sitting through sermons was as tough as trying to read books at school.

One morning, Gordon's attention quickly drifted from his father's sermon to masterly flipping his cap. In the front row. Right in front of his dad. Suddenly, young Gordon, miles away mentally from his surroundings, effected the Mother of All Flips. That cap went flying heavenward! By way of his dad's direct field of vision. The preacher's wrath was quick in coming earthward—down to the solitary figure seated in the front row. He stopped preaching.

Uh-oh.

"Take that away from him," the man behind the pulpit instructed Gordon's mother in measured tones.

Gordon swallowed hard. His mother reached into the pew before her and took the cap. Gordon then received a personalized sermon from the stern preacher. His father added more emphasis to the sermon when they arrived home later, too. That was the end of cap flipping in the sanctuary. Forever.

This was not the end of Gordon's troubled times in the confines of the church building, however. In his defense, he could hardly be blamed—he did spend more time there than most kids did. After an ill-timed, loud, affirmative "AMEN!" from Gordon's mouth during one of his father's sermons, he limited most of his amens to quieter benedictions after grace at mealtimes. That was a safer practice. And it didn't get him into trouble.

Sometime between the cap flipping fiasco and some

other Gordonian adventures, this busy PK did some exploring of their new homestead. They hadn't lived in this most recent house long and there was a lot of exploring that needed to be done. The parsonage was an old farmhouse that was connected to the barn—a convenient, if not aesthetically pleasing, arrangement.

Hmmm. Gordon scratched his head. No way into the old barn except through the big, heavy, sliding door that hung from an equally old track. He unlocked the securing hinges and proceeded to push the sizable partition between him and his awaiting New Adventure aside. He grunted and groaned with little headway. Suddenly, the door gave way.

The wrong way.

Instead of sliding on the track, it came off the track. Mr. Gravity did his part and the door began falling. Eager to get out of harm's way, Gordon made a mad dash away from the door to just inside the barn. The old wooden planks that made up the floor combined their talents with that of Mr. Gravity. Trip! Gordon went down! WHAM! The door followed! When the crash quieted and the dust settled, Gordon was trapped— with a badly broken leg—under the massive door.

His cries brought his mother to his aid. Once again, Dick was out of town. This time on an evangelistic tour. (It was one way for a preacher with a wife and four children to supplement his meager "ten dollars a week and all the potatoes you can eat" church salary.) Gordon's mother had to lift the door off her son, get him to the hospital, and then try to contact her husband. Gordon's memory of his leg being set is one he'd rather forget. He spent the next several weeks in a cast from his neck to his ankles. He didn't do much cap flipping, but he didn't have to scrape and paint pews or sit through church hour after hour for some time either.

The marvel of God's listening ear and special touch was apparent in this ordeal, too: Gordon has never had one minute of trouble with that healed fracture. He doesn't limp and the rainy weather doesn't irritate the early fractured femur.

Gordon didn't spend all his time in church or in the hospital or casted. Some of his activity was dictated by the climate in which they lived. The winters were so hard in their part of Maine that the children skated to school in the winter and put their shoes on once they arrived. It was safe to skate to school on the city streets —only skates and sleds could make their way down the slippery thoroughfares. Cars were left at home. Winters in Ottawa were mild compared to this part of Maine! Gordon and his family did not live in Maine for many more years, but his father continued in ministry in other New England states. In spite of their changing addresses and different schools, there were two constants in Gordon's youth. One of them was schoolwork.

Gordon would rather do *anything* than bury his face in a book. For good or ill, with the exception of the broken leg, he never missed a day of school. Thus he never missed out on his book learning.

Heavy sigh.

Spelling was the worst. Every misspelled word had to be rewritten ten times. Gordon had a *lot* of misspelled words. . .plus the ten new ones he had to learn for the next day. Life is tough when spelling words encroach on your free time! He was able to spell some words, however. He had no trouble spelling KICK ME I'M STUPID and sticking the sign on the organist's back one Sunday between the opening hymns and the closing song. There was only one thing that saved him from the wrath of the man in the cutaway coat that day. He told his father his buddy did it. (PKs learn to think fast on their feet.)

The other constant in the life of Gordon and his sisters was cod liver oil. Each one of the girls and Gordon got their daily dose of this dreaded liquid in all seasons and in every state where they lived. Their only hope of averting the gagging, oily substance was Mom or Dad developing amnesia. That almost *never* happened. Once it almost happened, but Gordon's error forever wiped out the possibility of it happening again. At least in the same way. . .

The family was hastily getting ready to go to the aforementioned organist's home for dinner. Dick had a flash of insight.

"Did you kids get your cod liver oil today?"

Groans all around.

"Gordon, go give your sisters each some and take some yourself."

They slowly and obediently tramped to the kitchen. Gordon grabbed a bottle out of the cupboard and gave his younger sister the first spoonful.

"YECH!" she exclaimed with a grimace. "That's bad!"

She carried on so much that their younger sister refused hers. She shook her head as Shirley continued complaining about the medicine, insisting it was worse than usual. Gordon looked at the label.

Liquid furniture polish.

Now he'd done it! Probably poisoned his sister! Gordon remembers his sister being violently ill all that day and the next. While he enjoyed the organist's delicious meal, poor Shirley spent most of the afternoon in the bathroom. She did survive the medicinal error, but she's never forgotten it. Nor has she let her brother forget it. It was the last time his father instructed Gordon to dispense any medicine.

Gordon had a few more years to go before he exited youth to the safe confines (for him, anyway) of adulthood. After another move or two, his family ended up in Connecticut. At church camp that summer, the camp was given a new archery set. This archery set was no toy. It was the real thing—semiprofessional, Gordon says, with a sixty-pound bow. The medical paranoia that characterizes our society today was still many years in the future. (So, apparently, was good common sense.) The camp counselors said anyone who wanted to try his or her hand at this archery thing was welcome to. The teenagers flocked to the adjacent "archery field," where they competed to be on teams. None of them had ever had a genuine bow and arrow in his hands before. This would be great fun!

Gordon took his try at it and actually hit the target. As the kids all waited to take their respective turns at playing Robin Hood, they stood around in groups talking. As Gordon talked with a circle of friends, a girl from his church tried her hand at the bow. She pulled the bowstring back a little too far and *WHIZ!* That arrow went *sideways* instead of straight. It flew past Gordon's face, the feathers glancing his eye. Trouble had found Gordon again.

When the camp nurse saw Gordon's eye, she knew they had a problem on their hands. She put salve on his eye, covered it, and got someone to take Gordon home *pronto*—in spite of Gordon's protests that he was all right. Complicating matters was the day of the accident;

it was over the Fourth of July holiday.

Again, because of the Lord's kindness in response to the fervent, believing prayers offered by Gordon's parents, a surgeon was located and Gordon had surgery the next day. The injury had been very serious in spite of the minimal pain. Gordon wasn't allowed out of bed for two weeks. The surgeon was skeptical that Gordon would retain sight in the injured eye. But his skepticism meant nothing to the greater Healer. Decades later Gordon can even read with the eye for which the physician had little hope.

Since Gordon met his lovely wife of over thirty years, he's been almost disaster-free. Neither has he almost poisoned anyone. (Although he did leave his two small daughters at church once and at a burger joint another time as well.) He's been in church ministry part-time or full-time his entire life, in spite of feeling like he was in church as much as a hymnal when he was growing up. Like his godly parents, who celebrated over sixty-five years of marriage in 1998, he has witnessed marvelous answers to prayer. Prayer was taught him by mouth, by example, and by his own life experiences with the One who both hears and answers prayer.

Gordon was a PK all right.

A Prayer Kid.

CHAPTER 6
God and Country

L ittle blond, blue-eyed Wilma snuggled up tightly against her grandfather. She rested contentedly on one of his knees. His well-worn Dutch Bible rested on the other. Many a night they spent like this: he reading a long passage from Genesis about Abraham, Isaac, or Jacob. She feeling the resonance of his voice in his chest, trying hard to understand all he was teaching her. He would translate into English for her as he went, asking her questions about what he read. She could understand her parents' and grandparents' native tongue in everyday conversation. She spoke Dutch conversationally herself. But here in the Bible? It was like a third language! But she could overlook the difficulties of Isaac and Rebekah and their troubles for the warmth and contentment of her grandfather's lap!

Wilma's father's family came from the Netherlands in 1910. Her mother's family came to America from the same country in 1923. Wilma's father, Tom, immigrated with his parents and brother and sister when he was just a boy. In "the old country," Tom's father, Louis, had been a drinking man whose ways made life a struggle for his family. That was before Jesus Christ took hold of Louis and changed him. Not long after this radical change in his life, the man who became what the Bible calls a "new creation in Christ" decided he and his entire family would start new in every sense of the word. Louis gathered his wife and three children around him and they came to America to begin afresh. Louis's son, Tom, was five years old when he set foot on American soil for the first time. That was how Wilma's father came to the U.S.

Passage from the old life to the new was much more traumatic for Wilma's mother, Dora, whose family did not immigrate until 1923. Dora was eighteen and in love when her parents made their decision.

"We are going to America," they announced.

Life had been hard in the Netherlands for them. All the crops Dora's father grew were confiscated by their unfriendly neighbors to the east. He had to work a second job to keep his large family from starvation. William had been told that the U.S. was a "land flowing with milk and honey." There was a large Dutch contingent living in Grand Rapids, Michigan. William had no idea where Grand Rapids, Michigan was, but the appeal of farming his own land without interference from enemies was an enticing lure. Wouldn't he like to take his family there?

The suggestion took root in William and his wife. His wife began knitting socks for all twelve children. She made them new traveling clothes as well. The boys helped with the knitting; it was a task shared by men and women alike in the Netherlands. They would all be going to America! The family began to prepare for their long sea voyage.

Dora did not share their enthusiasm. Yes, life was difficult, if not impossible, where they were. But the man she loved was here, in the Netherlands. Couldn't she stay with her grandmother?

Her father was adamant. They were a family. They would go to America as a family. Even the children who were older than Dora. Their entire family would emigrate. That concluded the discussion.

When their ship pulled into New York Harbor some months later, all the passengers flocked to the upper deck to see the Statue of Liberty. They cheered and waved in happy abandon! Dora stayed below deck, weeping for her lost love. There was no rush of joy or excitement for her in any of this.

Her parents had some genuine fears, however, as they went through customs. They had heard of other families who had crossed the ocean only to have some of their number denied entrance into their new land because of illness. Since Dora's mother was again expecting a child, each of the older children had been assigned one of the younger children to care for during the voyage. If any were found sick and denied immigration, the older child assigned to the younger would journey back to the Netherlands and their grandmother, leaving the rest of the family in America. That had been Dora's parents' decision before the journey. William was committed to staying in America and carving out a new life for his family.

He knew it was nothing short of a miracle when all fourteen of them were permitted to enter! They had no sponsors waiting for them. They spoke no English. Their new clothes, fashionable enough in the Netherlands, were *not* fashionable here in New York City! They *looked* like people who "had just gotten off the boat." They knew very little of this land to which they had come. They could not read signs or understand those around them. But here they were now—all together and entering their adopted country. *Together!* William, as head of his family, gathered them around him and prayed aloud in Dutch right there, thanking God for this miracle in their behalf.

That is how Wilma's "people," as she calls them, came to the United States. Surprisingly enough, Wilma's mother, the pining eighteen-year-old, became the most avid American patriot in the family. Sixty years later, when Wilma and her sister, Tena, decided to journey back to their roots in the Netherlands in the mid 1980s, Dora refused to go with them. There were too many bad memories there! America was her country! She would stay in America until she went to her heavenly home!

But that's getting way ahead of the story. . . .

The Dutch community that had settled in Grand Rapids was tight and close-knit. It was a given that everyone went to the local Christian Reformed Church. It was also a given that one did not marry outside one's people. To say this group of people was clannish would be an understatement. Louis and his family had settled in around 1910. Thirteen years later William and Dora arrived in this same community. They had set about immediately to get their own farm among their Dutch neighbors. William worked for another farmer. The older children, too, got jobs to work to that common end. Dora's mother took in laundry and ironing. Soon they had enough to buy their own farm once again.

In their small ethnic community, it wasn't long before Dora met Tom and they became the connecting link between Tom's small family and Dora's dozen. The young man Dora had left behind was soon forgotten. She and Tom married and started their own family. But a long period of lean years was hovering about the future's horizon for all of them, even here in their adopted country.

During the Depression, the men feared they would lose everything, particularly their homes. Since Tom's parents had the bigger house, he and Dora sold their house and moved in with Tom's mother and father. Wilma was born near the end of the Depression. However, the Depression's crippling, economic shock waves continued to reverberate throughout America. Wilma has no memory of life without her father's parents, Louis and Tena, living with them. That was not such an unusual arrangement then. In fact, there was nothing unusual about it at all. Except for Wilma's grandfather, Louis, who *was* somewhat unusual.

Louis was not unlike a reformed smoker who wages war against cigarette smokers, tobacco companies, and makers of ashtrays. He had been delivered from alcohol addiction and was zealous in his appeal to others to repent and live uprightly. Although he had only a third- or fourth-grade education, he never hesitated to butt heads with the teachers at the nearby Christian college or the professors at the local seminary. This hard-line, self-appointed preacher would take up his mantle and preach—to teachers, family, neighbors, or even church committee members. His approach to people made him a rather controversial member of their community. That was outspoken Grandpa! Louis was careful that his grandchildren got the message as well. That was how Wilma often ended up snuggled on her grandfather's lap, listening to him read from his well-worn Dutch Bible.

Wilma's life as a young child was a delightful blend of her unique Calvinistic heritage and growing up in an average American small town in the 1940s. Even before she could read or write, her father taught her catechism. He would ask his preschooler the questions, then help her memorize the answers. Family devotions were basic: prayer with every meal; the reading of a psalm every noontime; and the reading of another portion of scripture every night. The family did not discuss application of the Word to life, but Wilma's father always made the children repeat back to him the last few words of the passage he read. That was how he made sure they were listening!

Wilma, like others who grew up in strict Calvinist homes, was a "covenant child": She had been baptized as an infant and her parents had promised at her baptism to instruct her in the Word of God. Tom and Dora and their church would do their part in Wilma's religious training. They believed that God would do His part in redeeming her before the day of her death. This was the "covenant" Wilma's parents wholly believed in and claimed for each of their children. That was how and why Wilma, as a covenant child, was started in the Heidelberg Catechism even before she could read. Her parents took their part of this promise or covenant with God very seriously.

In many ways Wilma and her siblings were reared very legalistically. Sundays were special. Mother prepared the food on Saturday so she would not be working in the kitchen on Sunday. The family was in church two or three times on Sunday and the children stayed in their "Sunday clothes" in part to discourage them from playing as they did on other days of the week.

Cosmetics were out of the question! Even for church —especially for church! As the girls grew older, Wilma's oldest sister would put makeup on after she left the house to go out with friends. . .and remove it before she returned. If her parents found it, however, in the fire it went! If Mother could do without makeup, so could and *would* their daughters!

Their church services were held in both English and Dutch. Services were heavy with liturgy and the pulpit was a holy place. With few and rare exceptions, no one else stood or sat on the platform but the minister. Most of every Sunday was spent in church.

Wilma's father always worked hard to make ends meet. He usually worked two jobs. His year-round job was being the church janitor. With so much of their life centered in their church, Wilma and her siblings would often "play church." The neighboring children of Dutch families were not the only ones present. Other neighborhood children came to play with Wilma and her siblings as well. One young Jewish friend was shocked to hear "Preacher Doris," the role often assumed by Wilma's older sister, refer to their ethnic group as "the chosen people." Their little friend looked up, startled.

"*We* are the chosen people!" he declared. Wilma does not recall how the challenge was settled among them that day. But this son of Abraham was far outnumbered by these staunch Dutch Calvinists on this particular day of "playing church."

In the winter Wilma's father also delivered coal. Wilma remembers running excitedly to greet him, black as he was from head to foot except for his sparkling, piercing blue eyes. After cleaning up and sharing their evening mealtime, prayers, and scripture reading, her father would read *Uncle Wiggley* stories out of the newspaper to them before bedtime. With few books available to them around the house, this was homespun entertainment at its best!

Wilma has no memories of ever being in want or going hungry, yet she recalls one Christmas in the early 1940s when the "Santa Claus Girls" came to their house delivering gifts. Not only did they bring toys for Wilma and her sisters and brother, but oranges and other staples for the pantry. The best gift of all from her mother's viewpoint was some coffee! It was a treasure! The "Santa Claus Girls," part of a local charity, brightened up their Christmas considerably that year.

During these years Wilma had no understanding that day-to-day living for their multigenerational family was a matter of paying for everything "on time." Even groceries! The local small grocery store, where everyone who shopped there was known, knew its patrons were good for payment, sooner or later. And so Wilma's family, like others, managed from month to month and year to year—always in the red, but always paying for what they purchased as soon as possible.

Wilma has three crystal-clear memories concerning World War II. One is the blue stars and the gold stars in the windows of soldiers' homes. They even had a star-studded banner at church filled with blue and gold stars. During those days, each blue star represented a loved one serving in the U.S. military. Every gold star stood for one who had served and lost his life in the process. There were few houses without stars of one color or the other.

Then there were the blackouts! And the wardens! Americans were under no delusions about the war after Pearl Harbor. Bombs could be dropped in America just like they were being dropped in England and France. So, every town and city had regular drills: all lights out! The enforcers of these blackouts, the wardens, were people from every walk of life who would canvas their immediate neighborhoods and make sure everyone was in compliance. But for a little girl, these were protracted times of darkness when she simply wanted her mother and daddy close beside her.

Then in 1945, finally, came V-E Day and V-J Day. The war was over! Celebrations were not limited to big cities like New York and Chicago. In smaller cities and towns like Grand Rapids, everyone headed to town to celebrate! Wilma and all the children tied tin cans to their bicycles and rode them clang, clang, clanging through the streets in glad celebration! It was excitement the likes of which they had never seen! They didn't understand why their mothers were crying, but it was clear everyone was jubilant—even with the weeping! The festive atmosphere was contagious! Even the children understood: THE WAR WAS OVER!

It was a special year for Wilma in a private matter also—one that did not make the headlines on earth. It was the year she, like her grandfather before her, was confronted with the claims of Jesus Christ for her personally. Traditionally among her people, being born in a home like Wilma's was practically a shoe-in for one's entrance into heaven, at least from where they stood. Yet during Vacation Bible School a new young pastor who had come on staff at their church told the children of the importance of a personal commitment to Jesus Christ. Wilma was one of the children who received Christ as her personal Lord and Savior that summer.

Her parents, God-loving and God-fearing people, said little when Wilma made her announcement about how she "gave [her] heart to Jesus" that day. Hadn't she been brought up to believe in Jesus? Wasn't she a covenant child? Wasn't she still learning her catechism? What was this unusual method this pastor introduced? Was this *necessary* for a girl brought up correctly in a proper, God-fearing home? Had they not taught her to love and obey the Lord?

All these thoughts passed through their minds and from their lips when they talked privately in their Dutch tongue to one another about seven-year-old Wilma's declaration. They never spoke of it—good or bad—to Wilma. For Wilma, however, it sealed for all time her relationship with the One who loved and knew her before she was born.

Wilma has no regrets about her strict Calvinist heritage. There *was* legalism. But the Word of God was read to her daily, even after she could read it herself. And God's Word does its work, just as the Bible declares. It never returns to the Giver empty; it always accomplishes its sent purposes.

There was unabashed patriotism in their home. Wilma still remembers the side-by-side pictures in the living room. An artist's rendering of Jesus Christ hung next to a big photograph of Teddy Roosevelt.

Love was present in their home as well. It was the glue that held everything—and everyone—together. The patriotism of her grandparents and parents was exceeded only by their loyalty and devotion to God and to one another. That was the heritage they passed on to their children.

When she was older, Wilma once asked her mother why she always prayed in Dutch. Her mother, being a teenager when she came to America, always retained her heavy Dutch accent, although she learned to speak English fluently. Wilma had no understanding, however, of why her mother never prayed in English.

"Your father and I always spoke our 'sweet talk' in Dutch," her mother, Dora, answered. "I pray to God in Dutch because it is the language of my heart."

The always present but perhaps little-spoken under-girding love in Wilma's family was genuine. It did not have its origins in religion or in love of one country over another, but in the love of God. Legalism and patriotism always take a backseat to the Better Thing, the love of God taught and lived out in a stable, loving home.

And for Wilma and for most of us, the Better Thing is the Treasured Thing.

CHAPTER 7
Get It in Writing

Betty watched as her sister left the room to get the letters. Betty and her girlfriend Irene had made this cross-country journey to "see America" before they settled down. Irene, for the serious business of job hunting, and Betty, for the equally serious job of husband hunting.

The two young women had met in nursing school and become fast friends. Betty found she didn't have the stomach—literally—for nursing. The sounds (suction in the delivery room) and the smells (cauterization in surgery) put her facedown in the aforementioned arenas faster than anyone could yell: "We need smelling salts in here!" The untimely, abrupt end of her most recent clinical observation in surgery also marked the untimely, abrupt end of her nurses' training. Irene found Betty's swooning experiences hilarious; Betty found them frustratingly humiliating. She was helped out of the operating room with assistance. She left nursing school under her own power.

When Irene completed her nurses' training on the scheduled date, the two of them set off for California. This was to be their last fling as independent, unattached women. Today Irene was at the beach; Betty was spending some private time with her sister. The two friends had been persuaded (by a letter from Betty's sister) to stay with her and her husband when they came west. So, here they were.

It had been a peculiar few days. Betty grew up estranged from her birth family. She met her sister Blanche when her friend Irene met her: the day they arrived at Phil and Blanche's home for this visit. Her older sister and brother-in-law had made them feel very welcome, but Betty couldn't deny her discomfort. She and Blanche were more strangers than they were immediate family. Betty had known of Blanche but had never met her until a few days ago. She felt ill at ease, but both she and Blanche were committed to getting to know one another. They were sisters, after all, even though they had been separated for well over fifteen years. So Phil had gone off to work and Irene had returned for one more day at the beach. The sisters had a few hours to themselves; Betty's sunburn kept her away from the beach.

Blanche was taking advantage of their time alone to help her younger sister get to know another family member whom Betty would never have the opportunity to meet. Their brother Zollie had been killed in the war before Betty was reunited with her birth family. Blanche had (fortunately) saved all his letters to her.

"Here they are!" she announced as she returned to the kitchen. Pulling a chair closer to her sister's, Blanche laid the stack of letters on the table. She took a drink of her lemonade after she sat down.

"I am so glad I saved all Zollie's letters!" she said. "It's a better way for you to get to know what he was like than me simply talking about him." Their brother had been killed more than sixteen months ago. It was now the fall of 1946.

"This is the first letter I received from him as he was on his way to Europe," Blanche said.

Betty opened the letter, which was dated Monday, September 18, 1944. She tried to visualize the young man whom she had only known from some pictures shown to her.

> *This time [he wrote] I'm not in a train in the States [but] rather one of Uncle Sam's ships at sea. Yes, Sis, I figured after this war I had some brothers I would have to live with, and staying in the States for the duration of the war would have given me some uncomfortable moments. Now I will be able to compete in some of their conversations—I hope.*

Zollie went on in his letter to say that he had gotten to see his sweetheart before leaving and they became *"more in love than ever."* Yet his chance introduction to a beautiful young lady just prior to leaving the States was a complication he had not foreseen. He spoke glowingly, if not a little bashfully, of both women in his letter.

"Obviously," Blanche said with a small laugh, "all his thoughts weren't on the military!"

"I like what he says here about the 'swell orchestra on ship and the two swell piano players,'" Betty said. "I didn't know the army did so much for the men's convenience and entertainment!"

As she read on, it was clear that the army was still the army, however. He complained of having to read and censor the outgoing mail. He understood the necessity of it, he said, but he also found it frustrating to do —and to have it done to him! That was part of his responsibilities as they arrived and docked in England.

Betty picked up another letter and read of her brother's impressions of what he called "a bloomin' country, jolly ole England." But he clearly found France even more intriguing when he arrived on the continent. Although he wrote of the destruction of Caen, his lack of sleep (five hours in three days), and the rain and mud, he couldn't get over the welcome afforded them in France and then Belgium. Betty smiled as she read his very typical soldier account:

The people can't do enough for us, and such a mass of people all cheering with expressions of complete joy I have never seen before—'til I hit Belgium. Cigarettes and soap are about as hard to get as diamonds in the States. I understand cigs sell for $10 a package in Paris (500 francs) if available at all.

"No matter how often I wrote him," Blanche interjected as she and Betty continued to read over the letters together, "you can see he always asked for more. Sometimes I couldn't write as often as I wanted, but usually the problem was on his end. It would take weeks for my letters to catch up with him! They were constantly on the move. It was the same for all the soldiers, I guess. At least, that's what I understand him to say in this letter. Sometimes his letters were slow in coming to me, too."

Betty pointed to the six-cent postage stamp on the letter. "Well, it couldn't be for insufficient postage! He paid the full amount like everyone else!" She turned her attention back to the next letter while Blanche continued to speak.

"I couldn't help but think—even when I got this letter around Thanksgiving of '44—how different our situations were. I felt so safe here in California with Phil. And there was Zollie, right in enemy territory! You can see," Blanche said, pointing, "that this was his first letter from Germany."

Betty somberly read the neat cursive that was her brother's penmanship.

Information I can write and care to write about is quite limited. However I will write what I can and some things maybe I really shouldn't despite the fact I am allowed to. . . . I think you have an idea of an infantry man's life here. It isn't exactly what one would do for wanting to. I have a platoon of men. . .and usually I have at least a section of machine guns attached so when I do have a complete group, it would be 60 or better. . . . They keep me pretty busy. . . . I'm so proud of everyone. The American Infantryman is a man who one can really be proud of. . . .

Right now I am in my command post and have my plat sgt, msgr & medic with me as usual. Very good men. Our shelter is a hole dug about 4 feet deep and 12 ft. by 12 ft. Outside of the hole we have logs about 12" thick built around and over us. Especially over. We must have at least 2 or 3 feet of logs over us. It is quite a structure. Every crevice is closed so not even the tiniest speck of light from our candle can be seen, and we are thankful to see and have this place. It is lots of

*work, but you would be surprised how 3 men—
plus what help I could give when I had a few
moments—can erect one. We are really getting to
be quite the home builders, tho I must say to go
into the business when we get back, we would
have to change our design.*

"I liked reading this letter," Blanche said after briefly skimming it and handing it to her sister. "I could never get over how much the men over there knew of what was going on over here. Look at what he says here," she said, reading it aloud:

*I did get to hear about 2 innings of one of the
Series games. . . . I'm also a rabid football fan and
am sorry I missed some of the swell games this
year. There seems to be a lot of talk of Ohio State
playing in this year's Rose Bowl game. Look out,
SC, for Les Horvath.*

"Who's Les Horvath?" Betty asked.

"I don't know! We'll have to ask Phil when he comes home."

The two women continued to pore over the letters, reading between the lines as, just before Christmas, Zollie told of being twenty-six and feeling old compared to the rest of the men in his company. Betty noticed that he slipped into the third person when writing about getting the Purple Heart. He also wrote "your brother is to receive the Silver Star or a Bronze Star for something he did a few days back."

"I think things were starting to get bad for them," Blanche said quietly as her sister read. Her remark was absently addressed to the window rather than the person beside her, who continued her reading.

I could write more. . .but I don't have the time. That's what I got into when I became platoon commander of fifty men. I have to look out for everyone besides myself. Even tho I only have fourteen left, it is really enough to keep one busy. . . .

The past few days have been rough indeed. I lost some great men, but then we in the Infantry expect that. Myself I keep fighting. Got lots to fight for.

" 'Got lots to fight for,' " Betty quoted. "I wonder who or what he was thinking about."

"We'll never know," Blanche replied. She pulled the last letter from its envelope. "This is the last letter I got from him," she said soberly, handing it to her sister. "I often wonder if he had a premonition of what was coming. He even signed this letter differently from the rest."

Betty took the letter from her sister's hand. She

smiled a sad smile as the writer bragged on his Midwest girlfriend's knitting ability. He had received knitted socks and a sweater from her for Christmas. But Christmas had also dealt them some heavy blows. "Many familiar faces were missing," he wrote, "which kept away lots of our happiness." Betty had to wipe at the unbidden tear that had replaced her hint of a smile.

Guess I had better see how my men are coming along. I like the relief on their faces of the past few days. One thing about our American soldier. Take him out of the rough going places and the hardship and bitterness soon disappear from his face and he is soon smiling and forgetting.

"Amazing, wasn't it?" she said more to herself than to Blanche. "In the middle of all that and those men were still able to smile and put it behind them!" She read the last page of the letter slowly.

It's trees, snow, hills, flattened villages, and more snow. A beautiful winter day. Something very unusual however this a.m. I find myself with nothing to do but take life as I like. At least to a certain extent. I wouldn't exactly say I am living the life I love or love the life I live. I can truthfully say it is the life a frontline Yankee seldom has. I do not

*expect it to last, as no doubt I will soon be called
to adjust or fire artillery or possibly go over plans
for patrol. Keeping busy however does keep one
occupied and from thinking too deeply.*

Always Lovingly
Zollie

"He was killed in battle six days later," Blanche said
quietly as her sister put the letter down to wipe her eyes.

"He sounded like a wonderful man," Betty said, seeing tears glisten in her sister's eyes also.

"He was. You would have learned to love him as the
rest of us did. I will keep these letters for as long as I
live."

Keep them she has. Almost sixty years later, Blanche's
dearest treasures have been preserved on worn, yellowed
sheets of paper. In her possession she has the thoughts
and feelings of her younger brother, recorded by his
own hand, while he was in the middle of a battle he
would not escape.

There's something to be said for the days before fax
machines and typewritten electronic mail.

CHAPTER 8
Of Bengal Tigers and Such

If you were a young American male when December 7, 1941, dawned in Hawaii, there was no waiting to see if your "number came up." This was before the days of the military lottery of the 1960s. America was the Johnny-come-lately who became part of the world war that followed the world war to end all wars. American interests and safety were a little more clearly understood by the rank and file back then than the shades of gray that colored the battles fought more recently in places like Korea, Vietnam, or Kosovo. Americans stationed at Pearl Harbor in Honolulu had been attacked. War had come for the U.S.; it was the Allies versus the Axis powers. Overnight the Yanks were in the thick of it.

When people in the U.S. think of WWII, they probably think first of Pearl Harbor. Then Europe or the Pacific Islands come to mind: places like France, Germany, Guam, and the Philippines. But there were soldiers of both genders and all colors who were sent to places that did not garner the same headlines as the likes of Anzio or Normandy. Some of these men and women were sent to faraway, remote places like China, Burma, and India. Kenny was one of these men.

Kenny did not have to slop through water, sand, and rocks on a beachhead. He did not have to dodge bullets or dive into trenches ducking artillery fire. Like so many others, however, he had a job to do that was crucial to the Allies' war machine. He and numerous other GIs had their own wartime duties to bring anxiety to their minds and sweat to their bodies. Roads had to be built and aircraft landing strips had to be cut out of and through the jungle. There were pilots who had missions to fly in the Pacific. They needed fuel to fly and a place to get the fuel. It was the job of some of those in the "CBI theater" to transform jungle into airport. They did it under the intense Burmese sun and on land where powerful, less-than-friendly creatures cared little for these hardworking, sweaty Americans changing their topography. Speaking of topography, the land itself wasn't any too accommodating to the Allies' war effort either.

Clearing jungle for a warplane runway is hot, hard work in Burma. It's not only hot and hard, but it's dangerous work as well. The terrain is not easily judged beneath all that lush vegetation. War doesn't allow for a lot of time spent in classrooms learning the fine points of earthmoving equipment. It's that "old school" of learning rather than "Caterpillars and Crawlers 101, 102, and 103." The didactic instruction goes something like this: "There's the Cat. Here's the key. Get to work."

There wasn't time to waste in design or pedantry. There were planes coming in that needed refueling and needed it fast. The enemy could have already made a shambles of the landing strip just finished a week ago. The war effort in the Pacific needed men and it needed bombs. Men like Kenny made sure the pilots could get their planes down and refueled. So, unfriendly fauna and fowl notwithstanding, this group of soldiers cleared jungle.

Kenny's most vivid memory of this task was the day he rolled his Caterpillar. He was intent on what he was doing, but one side of the Caterpillar got hung up in the uneven terrain. It all happened so quickly that Ken had no time to escape from the powerful machine that began to topple over. He was trapped! Just as he expected to be crushed under the weight of the multiton monster he no longer controlled, he felt "someone grab me by my shirt collar." He was tossed (he clearly recalls making no effort of his own) well clear of the huge earthmover as it came crashing down, its treads spinning uselessly in the blistering Burmese sunshine.

Ken got up from the ground and stared at the upside-down Caterpillar with the others in his company. The One who had yanked him from the Cat-turned-wreckage was not visible, but Kenny knew Someone had saved his life. He knew it as well as he knew his name. But it would be many more years before this soldier gave himself to the God who had spared him from the mangled mess of metal that had been his earthmover. That "Ultimate Tap on the Shoulder" was still far in the future.

There was another cat Ken would have to grapple with before leaving Burma. But this one wasn't made of steel. It was alive. It was big. It was striped. It was whiskered. And it was mad. *Real mad.*

Two of the officers in Kenny's company had taken some free time to get away from the business of overseeing the clearing of airstrips to do some big game hunting. They hoped to bag something that would set eyes to envying and tongues to wagging. Imagine their excitement when these two officers and gentlemen spotted a Bengal tiger! Bengal tigers are six feet long. Add the tail and there's nine feet of jungle cat! Bringing down a Bengal tiger would be something to write home about! And their skeptical fellow officers back at camp? Wait until they saw this! They took aim and fired away, there in the Burmese thicket.

Amazingly enough, these two ol' boys did get their

tiger. The good news was they brought it down in spite of being neophytes at this big game hunting thing. The bad news was they then had to get the tiger carcass back to camp. Not having the strength or inclination to load their five-hundred-pound-plus prize onto their jeep, they *dragged* the beast back to the compound behind the jeep. This was a rather inglorious end for a carnivore as powerful and commanding as a Bengal tiger—and a pretty dumb thing to do for two Americans who knew nothing about fragrant, ferocious felines. The scent of a female Bengal tiger—alive or dead—is a potent aroma, especially if you happen to be the sniffing male counterpart. These two GIs had dragged the poor female tiger for miles behind their army jeep. They left a direct Path of Fragrance from Point of Kill to Point of Army Compound for the male cat.

The fellow officers and soldiers may or may not have been impressed with the game hunters' bounty. One thing was for certain. They were *not* impressed with the way the tiger slayers brought the tigress home. After the first night of the hunters' arrival back at base, large tiger tracks were found around the company sleeping quarters. The CO knew there could be trouble. *Everybody* knew there could be trouble. It was one thing having a man almost crushed under a big, steel Cat. It was quite another to be hunted by a flesh-and-blood cat—fanged, clawed, and in poor humor. This bad boy of the jungle had logged some serious miles following the scent of his female counterpart. There was no happy feline reunion. He had looked for her and not found her. This male cat had just lost his mate to two neophyte big game hunters. He was in no mood for an attitude adjustment. He who had been one of the hunted became the hunter. The stalked became the stalker.

The officer in charge made a decision. He posted a guard for the camp at night. Kenny was the one selected to keep vigil. The rolled Caterpillar survivor took his army-issued rifle, was given a powerful spotlight, and had a chair constructed not unlike that of a lifeguard's. This was the perch from which he could watch for the tiger, should he return again. And it was expected the tiger would return again. No one in the group of soldiers wanted to match wits with a Bengal tiger, especially an unhappy Bengal tiger. But Kenny grew up hunting. He took the assigned task in stride.

The first night of watch came and went. Nothing happened.

The second night of watch came and went. Nothing happened.

"Forget it, Kenny," his commanding officer said the next morning. "I think the cat belonging to those tracks is long gone. I don't think we need to worry. He won't be back."

Ken wasn't so sure. He told his CO he had "a feeling

about this cat."

"I'll watch one more night," he said. The officer shrugged his shoulders in deference to Kenny's instincts. So for one more night Kenny climbed up and seated himself in his jungle perch.

The Burmese night was as black and quiet as the day was bright and noisy. Kenny sat patiently in his chair, occasionally smoking a cigarette, listening for any sound out of the ordinary. Then he heard it.

Snap!

Guess who had come to dinner?

And he wasn't looking for C rations.

Just the faintest crackle of splitting underbrush had put all of Kenny's senses on immediate alert. His muscles tensed and his adrenaline pumped. He reached soundlessly for the spotlight with one hand and for his rifle with the other. He pointed the spotlight in the direction of the noise and flipped the switch.

There he was! One-quarter ton of crouching, snarling, salivating bad attitude!

Kenny raised his rifle, took aim, and pulled the trigger.

CRACK!

Instant pandemonium! Soldiers in every combination of dress and undress (mostly undress, truth be told) came running full tilt out of their tents! Half asleep, sure they were under attack, stumbling over their weapons, throwing their helmets on their heads, they all dove for cover! During a war in the middle of the night, gunfire means only one thing: attack! And nobody was counting the number of gunshots.

Not one GI remembered the expected Bengal tiger or the lone soldier waiting for him. Kenny could hardly enjoy his triumph in bringing the big cat down with a solitary shot. He was too busy laughing at the chaos around him! There was no telling this group of panic-stricken soldiers that there had only been one bullet fired at one angry tiger. Until he could stop laughing and the dust had settled again, Kenny could only watch from his constructed perch above all the confusion. Not a few sheepish GIs stuck their heads up from the trenches moments later, puzzled by the silence.

This tale was long in the telling. The GIs talked and laughed about it and each other for days. They slapped Kenny on the back for bringing down the huge predator with a single shot and little light. Ken wrote about the incident to his mother. He told it to his friends when he came home from the war. He told it to his growing children. He repeated it good-naturedly to his skeptical sons-in-law who said almost every holiday more than fifty years after the war: "Tell us about the Bengal tiger again, Dad!"

Kenny's life was one intricately associated with cats of all kinds. He had stories to tell of pet cats, *Caterpillar* earthmovers, and Bengal tiger cats. But one of his favorite stories came to be of a different kind of "cat" altogether. C. S. Lewis called this Cat "Aslan." The Bible calls Him the Lion of the tribe of Judah.

More than twenty years after the Lord Jesus Christ rescued Kenny from certain death beneath a steel Cat in Burma and possible death from the attack of a Bengal tiger, He rescued him from the roaring lion who seeks to destroy us all.

Leave it to God to weave the threads of a man's life together in an uncommon, colorful tapestry!

CHAPTER 9

Assignment: Anzio

I've decided to go into nursing, Grandma."

Elsie looked up in surprise at Laura. Her granddaughter resembled her at that age: dark, curly hair, an enviable complexion that needed no cosmetics, and eyes the color of the sea on a cloudless, sunny day.

"Nursing! I thought you wanted to be a teacher!" Elsie was more than surprised at this revelation.

Laura sat down beside her on the sofa, reaching for a photo album that Elsie had been going through the previous evening. "Tell me about the pictures in this album of yours. I found them so interesting, but I have so many questions! I thought you were just in Italy during World War II."

"I was in Italy part of the time but not the whole time," Elsie informed her.

"Look at you in this picture, Grandma!" Laura pointed and giggled. "Did you have to wear your hair like that?" She didn't give her grandmother time to answer. "And this picture of you and your friends! What about this dilapidated tent here? I want you to tell me about these pictures. I want you to tell me about nursing during the war. Did you always want to be a nurse?"

Laura's questions came out in such a rapid, jumbled succession that Elsie hesitated before answering. She didn't know which one to answer first! She pushed one shoe off and then the other as she got comfortable next to her granddaughter.

"From the time I was four years old, I wanted to be a nurse," she said, clearly remembering the last asked question.

"Really? I think I wanted to be an Olympic ice skater when I was four!" Laura returned, bringing her legs up onto the love seat. "How long did it take you back then to finish nursing school?"

"I graduated from high school when I was sixteen and from nursing school when I was twenty."

"No kidding! That's the age I'll be if I get an associate degree in nursing!"

"Well," Elsie said, smiling at the eager high school senior beside her, "in the 1940s one could not take the state nursing boards until she was twenty-one. So I had to wait a year. But I wanted to go into army nursing, too. I wanted to go overseas."

"Tell me about it, Grandma. We've got the afternoon

and these pictures to help me 'see' your story. I want to know all about it!"

Looking at the full album of faces and places from long ago, Elsie started at the beginning. To the days when she wanted to be a nurse, but never an army nurse!

Throughout her first years in nurses' training, Elsie considered herself a pacifist. She was certain, therefore, that she would never become an army nurse. As a senior nursing student, however, she was assigned to work for two months with a visiting nurse. In the course of their conversation one day, Elsie expressed her opinion on the topic of military nursing. It was a natural topic for an idealistic nursing student and a somewhat less idealistic, experienced nurse—particularly in the middle of World War II. The older nurse listened respectfully to Elsie's point of view and then made a simple, nonjudgmental statement.

"You took an oath to help heal others," she said firmly. "Regardless of the cause."

Elsie thought about those words while she waited to take her board exams. They kept coming back to her in the weeks and months that followed. By the time she had successfully passed her exams, she had made her decision. She became an American Red Cross nurse. From there she stepped into military nursing as an army officer. When Elsie joined the Army Nurses Corps, foreign service for nurses was strictly voluntary. She would have more time to think about going overseas. Bombs and bullets were not selective in the war zone. Putting oneself in harm's way *voluntarily* was a sobering thought. Overseas service duty was serious business indeed. Elsie considered all this and more as she began her initial service training.

She did not have long to consider her options. Two weeks after Elsie became an army nurse, the army abruptly reversed its position. All army nurses would have to do a tour of overseas duty. Starting immediately. Elsie's decision had been made for her. In her heart of hearts, she had decided it was what she really wanted to do and felt called to do. She was ready to take her place "helping to heal" those who needed it most.

After Elsie's initial duty at Nichols General Hospital in Louisville, Kentucky, she was assigned to the 105th Station Hospital being formed at Fort Knox. In the spring of 1943 the 105th boarded the *Edmund B. Alexander* at Staten Island, New York. Elsie's excitement knew no bounds! Here she was, twenty-two years old and heading for North Africa! She couldn't wait for the adventure and challenge of her new career and profession in a foreign country! She would be helping make a difference in a world wracked by war!

She had been in the army for less than six months. She had been in nursing for less than two years.

From the time she boarded ship, she knew she was in for an adventure like no other. Even the ship had a history! It was an old, hulking Irish vessel that had seen action in World War I. The Germans had captured it, changing its name from the *Halifax* to the *Fatherland*. The ship's story, passed from crew to passengers, went on to say that the United States in turn captured the ship from the Germans and renamed it the *Edmund B. Alexander*. This old vessel had seen many years and a lot of war, but it was still regarded as seaworthy. Elsie and her crewmates felt very safe as they crossed the Atlantic. A convoy of over thirty ships surrounded them. As protected and safe as they felt, however, the fact remained that lifeboat drills were still a necessary part of life aboard ship during wartime. The nurses generally slept in their clothes, anticipating the inevitable, routine, middle-of-the-night drills.

At three o'clock in the morning on May 8, 1943, there was no drill. An explosion onboard roused them from sleep! Certain they had been torpedoed by an enemy submarine, the nurses nervously sat in their berths, their lifejackets on, awaiting orders to proceed to the lifeboats. Questions ran through Elsie's head rapid-fire. Had the other ships in their convoy been hit? Was there one renegade submarine who had targeted them? Where were the destroyers in their company?

Would they all die at sea before ever reaching their destination?

All these thoughts and others fired the nurses' adrenaline and spirited their prayers heavenward. But soon their worst fears were quieted. They never had to board the lifeboats. The explosion was not from enemy fire, but from the old *Edmund B. Alexander* blowing an engine under the strain of trying to keep up with the newer, faster vessels in its company. Thankfully, no one was injured or killed, but the old Irish-built ship and its passengers had to be left behind to proceed at a slower speed. They were escorted the remainder of their trip to Africa by two sentinel destroyers.

The rest of their trip was uneventful. They lacked the safety in numbers that they had had during the first part of their journey, but they put into safe harbor at Gibraltar. They finally arrived at their destination in North Africa, but it was some days later than originally planned.

"Wow, Grandma! I never knew you almost got blown away at sea!" Laura said. "And you went to Africa? Africa-Africa?"

Elsie had to laugh. "North Africa, honey. North Africa saw a lot of World War II also." She shifted her position and pointed to one of the pictures. "I was in North Africa for ten months. Some of the time was in

Algeria and some of it in Tunisia. We had some unforgettable experiences in Africa! Some of it had to do with nursing, some didn't. But it was all tied up with being in the military!"

In Ain-Mokra, Elsie remembered, an August forest fire almost destroyed the surgery tent hospital and the medical rest tents. As the fire raged closer, everyone was instructed to take what he or she valued most out of their tents. It did not look like any of the tents would be spared from the approaching inferno. Elsie gathered up her pictures and her daily diary. Those were her most valued treasures. God intervened, however. Evacuation was not necessary. The fire was contained before it reached them, but the near-disaster had been far too close for comfort. All the local people, the patients, and the military personnel breathed sighs of relief. Elsie was quickly learning that there would be nothing ordinary or routine in her life as an army nurse!

Not long after the fire, Elsie and all the rest of the hospital personnel had to take a train ride across northern Africa. This unforgettable journey was made on an English-style narrow-gauge railroad. Elsie's five-day, four-night train ride from Ain-Mokra to Ferryville introduced her and the rest of the 105th Station Hospital nurses to cramped living quarters. And bedbugs. Six women were assigned to a two-person berth. These berths, or compartments, consisted of two benches with an aisle between them. One nurse slept in a fetal position at one end of the bench and another nurse sat tightly scrunched at the opposite end until it was her turn to assume the lying-down fetal position (as opposed to the sitting-up fetal position). The transition took place midway through the night. Same thing on the other bench in the compartment. Between these four unfortunates, nurse number five slept on the floor between them. The last nurse in this cozy sextuplet slept in the aisle outside the full compartment, a white towel as a protective pillow under her head. The white towel served a dual purpose. It was clean bedding between the nurse's head and the floor of the car. It was also a bright reminder to any person stumbling her way through the car at night that a head was there.

"Apparently other body parts were considered expendable!" Elsie said with a laugh.

"How did you stand it, Gran?" Laura asked, her expressive eyes wide with disbelief.

"Oh, that wasn't the worst of it! The worst snag in this otherwise blissful excursion was the creepy-crawlies! We had been given cans of powder before we got on the train because, we were told, 'the bedbugs are really bad.' "

"Gross!"

"It was gross," Elsie agreed. "We weren't quite sure what to do with the powder, so we had sprinkled it on the bedbug-infested bedding. That was the wrong thing to do! The bedbugs left their powdery dwellings and set up housekeeping on us."

"That," Laura said with emphasis, "is disgusting!" She shuddered. "What else do you remember about Africa, Grandma?" she asked, eager to leave the subject of bedbugs.

"Christmas there. I remember my one and only Christmas in Africa."

Christmas in Africa was difficult for Elsie. She had letters from home, gifts from home, and she wasn't near the front, but an unexplainable depression settled over her. She was doing what she wanted to do and content where she was, but the black cloud would not disperse. She couldn't understand it and didn't know what to do about it. Again, God intervened in her life in an unusual way.

One walk over to the hospital on Christmas Eve brought the silver lining Elsie needed. The patients had used everything available to make colorful paper chains with which they decorated—floor to ceiling—their Quonset hospital. The staff didn't know how these recuperating men managed to get the yards and yards of gaily-colored chains strung the width and length of the hospital, but they didn't need to know. They simply marveled in the wonder and simple, hand-wrought beauty of it and enjoyed their first and last Christmas together in Africa. Elsie's depression disappeared! If these injured, sick, and ailing men could do this for them, how could she be depressed? It was a memorable Christmas, but the demands and difficulties of army nursing in North Africa were only a prelude to what was coming. . . .

In February 1944 a dozen nurses from Elsie's unit, the 105th Station Hospital, received their orders. The Anzio beachhead had been established in January. Elsie and a small number of other nurses were going to join the hospitals there on detached service. Six nurses had been killed in the early weeks of the Anzio offensive and others wounded. Replacements were needed.

"So that was how you got to Italy," Laura interjected.

"That was how we got to Italy," Elsie said affirmatively, looking at the picture taken just before she went to Anzio.

Elsie and her group were flown to Naples, Italy, away from the relative calm of North Africa. They would be going into the middle of some of the fiercest fighting in Europe. From Naples the nurses boarded a British hospital ship, the *St. Andrews*. They were on their way to the Allies' Anzio front in southern Italy. They would be joining the troops who were going to push the Nazi army out of Rome. Anzio, thirty miles southeast of Rome, had become a strategic battlefield. The beachhead was about eighteen miles long and nine miles wide at its greatest depth. The Nazis surrounded this stretch of land completely on the north, south, and east. They were "dug into the hillside" and could observe every move the Allies made. Coming *and* going. There had already been a lot of fighting in the one month since the Allies had begun their invasion. It would continue to be a bloodbath for both sides. This was Elsie's destination as the *St. Andrews* made its way across the choppy waters of the Mediterranean. There was no turning back.

From ten o'clock in the morning until two o'clock in the afternoon, the Germans, by agreement, gave the Allies bomb-free time to evacuate their wounded. In the rough seas, the patients were brought to the *St. Andrews* on an LST (Landing Ship, Tanks). The tedious, time-consuming, stomach-lurching process dictated that one patient at a time, fitted in a shallow rectangular box, be raised manually by pulley from the LST to the ship. Once the sailors had pulled the patient onboard, he was taken out of the box. Two nurses were then seated, one in each end of the box, and transferred over the side of the ship and onto the LST. From here Elsie and the rest of the nurses were taken to shore. Once onshore, Elsie and the others were rapidly rushed to a waiting truck. With their belongings thrown in hastily alongside them, Elsie and two other nurses were driven to the Thirty-third Field Hospital. The other nurses in their group were assigned to evac hospitals in the immediate area. Elsie had begun what would turn out to be four long months right in the middle of World War II. They had not gone very far when the shelling started.

It was exactly two o'clock in the afternoon.

"So what did you have to do first when you got there?" Laura asked.

"Our education to the front lines was rapid and intense. The first order of business was to get our foxholes dug for the three new nurses. My cot was placed into my foxhole beneath my tent. Like the others, I was instructed to sleep with my helmet on. Good for protection —not so good for sleeping. When the rain started our first night there, the dirt plop, plop, plopping off the sides into the accumulating water beneath my cot, I could think of only one thing: *What in the world am I doing here?*

"But I thought of the soldiers who had no tents over them and I quickly pushed aside any lapse into a pity party."

The next day the nurses got trenches around their tent for drainage. While the trench got dug, Elsie received her duty assignment: six tents with forty cots. She had one corpsman per tent to help her in her care of the 240 patients under her charge. Each cot was equipped with three blankets: one to lie on, one for covering, and one to serve as a pillow. When a patient left, the blankets were shaken out and put back on the cot for the next man.

All the nurses worked twelve-hour shifts, seven days a week. Occasionally a nurse would become ill; then a working day became a twenty-hour day—or longer. Food supplies were scarce. Midnight lunches for the working staff showed little variety: Spam and coffee, cake and coffee, doughnuts and coffee. Patients came first in the "food chain," enlisted men second, and officers last of all when food was in short supply.

"We had plenty of medical supplies, but we were always hungry," Elsie said wistfully. "Always hungry." Laura remained still as her grandmother's look lingered at a time she could not see and spoke so softly she had to strain to hear her. "It was not about to get better soon either."

On March 22, 1944, the hospitals were hit during a nightly shelling. Five patients were killed, eighteen were wounded. Elsie had never known such heartbreak. It was a horror that would be repeated in the weeks and months to come. It would always be a mystery to Elsie that the Nazis would grant the Allies time to evacuate their wounded in broad daylight, yet bomb the already injured who lay in the easily identified tent hospitals at night. Often the daytime shelling began whenever a group gathered for meals or church services. As a result, the officers were divided into two groups and the mess hall into three areas. In this way, it was hoped they would avoid losing all their senior staff should the mess hall take a direct hit when filled at mealtimes. The nighttime air raids remained the worst, however.

The patients who were able would roll off their cots onto the ground for protection. The nurses were instructed by the commanding officer to move around as little as possible. They would sit huddled in a corner of the nurses' station, hugging their knees, unable to stop shaking. Although their bodies told them they were frightened almost to death, their minds were amazingly calm and ordered, ready to attend to the needs of their patients.

One day as Elsie attended to the needs of her patients, a bomb hit.

"One second I was standing, the next I was facedown in the dirt! I didn't know how I got there!" she told her granddaughter. "When the shelling stopped, I told one of the soldiers I didn't know how I'd ended up on the floor. 'I pushed you!' he said, laughing at me."

"I can't imagine you sprawled on the floor, Gran—especially a dirt floor!"

"Well, I was and glad to be, too! We always watched out for each other! We had to!"

As the Americans and British troops slowly but persistently gained control of the Nazi-held countryside, the push toward Rome heightened in earnest. Elsie found herself with 275 new patients. The excess number of patients had been placed in the chaplain's tent.

She was given extra corpsmen to help attend the wounded, but she still found herself more than busy identifying patients with immediate, life-threatening injuries, those with profuse bleeding who needed transfer to a shock ward, and men needing pain or tetanus injections. She went methodically but briskly from injured man to injured man, taking care of their needs as best as she could with their limited personnel resources.

"So often I would ask a wounded soldier if he needed something for pain and he would reply, 'Don't worry about me, nurse. Take care of someone who is worse.' " The memory brought tears to her eyes. "I can't tell you how many times I heard that—and heard it from men who were clearly in a lot of pain themselves."

"Just like you said, Grandma. Always watching out for each other," Laura said, taking her grandmother's hand.

Elsie smiled at her granddaughter, glad for her sensitivity and maturity in spite of her youth. "It gave me courage to do what had to be done, even when the task was overwhelming.

"On May 28, the Tenth Field Hospital took over our location. The Thirty-third Field Hospital had begun operating as a true field hospital and less of an evac hospital, which is what we had been doing in our first months at Anzio. The field hospital, made up of three platoons, followed the front line of soldiers. As the front line advanced, the third platoon would "leapfrog" over the other two, keeping up with the advancing front line. Three doctors, eight nurses, and a number of corpsmen made up each platoon. Often we moved daily. I made up penicillin from its powdered form to mix it with sterile water for injection. The other nurses and I started IVs, a practice that, up until this time, had been reserved for physicians. For days we continued our leapfrogging maneuver as we came closer to Rome, following directly behind the front line."

Gas gangrene was a fact of life and its pernicious presence brought suffering and death on a daily basis. Now operating in a true field hospital arrangement, each platoon, including Elsie's, had a capacity for thirty patients.

"In one day we lost six of our thirty patients. I was twenty-three and had never seen so much death. I think my face must have resembled the faces of some of those six who died. We had worked and were working so hard! And still the men were dying! 'What's the use?' I thought." She looked at Laura, who was as caught up in hearing her story as she was in telling it. "The major must have read my mind. He came up to me at one point that day and said, 'If we weren't here, Elsie, none of these men would make it back to the evac hospital. Not one.'"

"I'll bet that helped you keep going," Laura said.

"Yes, it did. On June 4, 1944, the Fifth Army entered Rome. Rome was free from Nazi control! Three days later the hospital was moving with the advancing troops. A few of my friends and I were able to see the city, which, unlike many cities in Europe during the war, was still quite intact. Signs and banners stretched across the streets and read (in English): WELCOME TO THE AMERICANS! or WELCOME TO THE LIBERATORS!

"Happy people flooded the streets of the age-old city. We were thrilled to be a part of it all. Indirectly, we had had a part in Rome's liberation! We reveled in sightseeing and walking about freely. We even did a little shopping. The only thing I remember buying was a pair of silk hose."

"Silk hose? You mean nylons?"

"No nylon hose then, honey. Our silk stockings were just that."

"Weird!" exclaimed Laura. She had never heard of silk stockings!

"After all the bombs and blood and heartache, I enjoyed those few hours of relative freedom with abandon. The officers who had dropped us off at the MP station for our carefree day returned later to pick us up as planned. We three nurses rode back to the hospital content. The Anzio beachhead campaign had been successful: Rome was free!"

Following the success of the Anzio campaign, late in

June Elsie and the rest of her small group were returned to the 105th Station Hospital. She remained in Italy until January 1945. The 105th set up their hospital at Grossetto, Civitavecchia, and Pisa, Italy. Elsie and other nurses like her who were nearing the end of their two-year overseas assignment were given two options. They could sign up for temporary duty, which meant thirty days stateside and then a return to the 105th, or they could sign up for rotation. Rotation meant thirty days in the U.S. and then one of two possibilities. The nurse could be assigned to remain in the U.S., or she could be assigned to another unit. Anywhere. "Anywhere" was not appealing; one could find herself easily in the Pacific theater. The Pacific was rumored among them to be the worst place to be assigned. Elsie decided to take her chances; she signed up for rotation.

"I was fortunate. My name was drawn and I was assigned to duty at home in the U.S.! I met your grandpa in New York City since he was stationed at Floyd Bennet Field in Brooklyn. We got married and, instead of going away for our honeymoon, we went *home* for our honeymoon!"

"And then you were done with being an army nurse?" Laura asked, turning the last page of her grandmother's album.

"Almost. I finished at Tilton General Hospital in Fort Dix, New Jersey. I was made a first lieutenant in

September of '44 and was honorably discharged the next year."

"Boy, Grandma, you sure have a story to tell!" Laura said with admiration.

"Still think you might want to go into nursing?" Elsie asked quizzically.

Laura thought a moment. "Yeah, I think I do. I may never have a story to tell like yours, but then again," she gave her grandmother a kiss on the cheek, "maybe I will."

Elsie traced the worn edge of her photo album with her finger as Laura went to the kitchen. Soon Elsie would meet again, just like she had every year since World War II ended, with the men and women with whom she served in the 105th Station Hospital. Again they would all be gathering to share laughter and tears. They would share pictures of new grandchildren and great-grandchildren and boast on the accomplishments of their sons and daughters. They would doubtless be smaller in number this year than last, but they would continue to remember together: how God used them, how much they endured, how they made a difference—and they would be content in the knowing.

CHAPTER 10
GI Joe

Joe would be moving today. His gait had become unsteady and he had taken a number of nasty falls of late. Once he must have been knocked out cold. He couldn't remember exactly where he was or just what had happened when he came to with the worried face of his neighbor peering down at him, assuring him the rescue squad was on the way. So, it was time to move into one of those assisted living places. That's what his son told him and he had had to agree.

"Is that everything?" his daughter-in-law asked, plopping down a box full of toiletries and medications. She dropped onto the sofa next to the overflowing box.

"I guess it is," Joe replied. He waved a small piece of paper he held in his hand at her. "Look at this! An old passport of mine!"

She took it from him and looked at it with interest. "Wow, Dad, this was a while back!"

"Don't I know it!" he agreed with a chuckle. "You know, I went back to Europe long after World War II ended to see what I could find of the places I'd been, and to look up some people I'd met. Funny I would go back to a place I had so dreaded going to in the first place!"

"You don't have a lot of fond memories of the war, do you, Dad?" she asked, handing the passport back to her father-in-law. He drew it up close to his face in order to see it. He'd often said to his son and his son's wife that he'd lived long enough that "blind in one eye and can't see out of the other" described him fairly accurately. He only had partial sight remaining in one eye, and that leftover part left a lot to be desired.

"Nope," he answered his daughter-in-law. "Just one. From the time I tried to join the U.S. Navy in 1941, I didn't have a good feeling about the war. I was sure there was a bullet out there with my name on it."

As the war intensified for U.S. troops, Joe knew it was only a matter of time before the draft board summoned him to knock on their door and sign on the dotted line. In spite of his apprehension, however, Joe thought he would beat the army at their own game. He went to enlist in the navy.

Joe's molar occlusion turned out to be his naval exclusion. It was something with which he was born. It had never given him a day's trouble. It was news to him that he even had this "molar occlusion," whatever it was!

But the navy was choosy, apparently, even when it came to something as seemingly incidental as teeth. Joe found himself facing the probability of being drafted again. It was a fact of life for young, single, healthy American men then. He decided he wouldn't wait for his draft notice. He went to the local draft board and signed up.

"They took anybody and everybody! We even had a guy in our outfit who didn't have a trigger finger!"

"No trigger finger! What did he do then?" his daughter-in-law asked, interrupting his tale.

"He passed out ammunition to those who did— have trigger fingers, that is." He smiled as his son's wife laughed. "They always found something for you to do," he said with emphasis.

Once Joe donned his army fatigues, he was sent first to England. Reality began to settle in when, during a close call in the midst of a bombing raid, Joe realized the Nazis were after him, too—not just the Brits, not just the French. But Americans as well. The Japanese Imperial Army was not the only enemy America was fighting in the early 1940s.

Joe hopscotched from England to Ireland and back to England again before being sent to France. As a combat soldier, he had a number of assignments that one quickly associates with the war in Europe: Normandy, Utah Beach, Omaha Beach. His dismal foreboding about the entire war was realized when he was issued an item every combat soldier carried on his person: his own body bag.

"That told you that you were expendable," he says with finality. He understood the practicality of it, but at the same time, carrying his own body bag on his *living* person gave him a feeling of impending doom. It suggested to him that he would not be a "living person" very long. As a result, Joe's lifestyle began a subtle (at first) pattern of self-destruction. He began drinking alcohol at every opportunity. When he didn't have an opportunity to go drinking, he often managed to make one. It got him into trouble on more than one occasion. The war was heavy, intense, and offered no relief for him and others who were being shot at day after day after day and were thousands of miles from home. The war was at its peak; Joe was in the middle of it. He always felt less than a step away from death. This oppressive obsession drove him not to his knees, but to the bottle. But he continued to fight on. That was all that was to be done for it.

After the Allies managed to break through the Nazi hold on Normandy, Joe was once again on the move with his company. But his stay at Omaha Beach, where he assisted in getting supplies into the area, was short-lived. There was more trouble brewing. Big trouble, close by. He was reassigned yet again. This time to Belgium.

The Germans were firing buzz bombs on Antwerp in Belgium. Antwerp was a significant port for bringing in supplies to the Allies. Thus, it became a primary target for the Germans' new robotic bombs. Dozens and dozens of these unmanned bombs, loaded with fifteen hundred pounds of firepower each, were fired from Germany into Belgium. Very state-of-the-art and deadly, these robot bombs were incredibly swift. Two or three of the flying bombs could be fired in rapid succession, making detonation by American counterfire little more than luck. If the American cannon fire did hit a buzz bomb, the bomb generally exploded on impact. The trick was to hit it. Joe was one of the men assigned to Belgium to intercept the buzz bombs before they made it to their destination.

Joe was given a prototype to work with as well. It was a computer composed of eighty vacuum tubes—no solid-state electronics, no microprocessors, no microchips. But this four-foot-square monstrosity, once programmed with a trial shot, controlled the cannon fire that brought down the buzz bombs—accurately and efficiently. The accuracy of Joe's early computer exceeded anything the men could do manually. Unfortunately, *where* the debris came down was not a factor the Americans could control. Both the Flemish people living in the area and Joe and the rest of his company were about to learn this lesson the hard way.

When Joe and his computer-controlled cannon hit one of his targets, the resulting inferno would light up the sky with a dazzling display of explosive fire. But not every Nazi buzz bomb exploded in midair. One "wounded" bomb glided out of the sky one day, just short of the local hospital. The implosion pulled the entire façade off one side of the building. A mother and her newborn infant were two of the casualties.

"The local people were incensed! The Nazis had been bombing them and now the Americans were doing essentially the same thing!"

"I'll bet that made for increased tension between you and the Flemish."

"It sure did. Any hero status we had initially went up in smoke when that hospital got the fallout from the intercepted buzz bomb. We were just another occupying army making their lives more miserable."

Aside from the inability to control where the fallout from successive hits would fall from the sky, Joe had no illusions about this assignment in Belgium. He was convinced he and his company would be there in Belgium for at least two years. If they lived that long. If *he* lived that long. He personally didn't think he'd survive the war. As a result, his drinking persisted as a daily fact of life. Between the drinking and his fatalism, Joe became surly and contentious. Little things would make him ready to fight—not just the Germans, but his own comrades.

One day he was working on one of their weapons on a gun platform. The censoring officer came to Joe, telling him he wrote nice letters. He thought they were so nice that he did more than read them over for purposes of censoring.

"I've been copying some of them and then sending them to my girlfriend," he admitted.

Joe was ready to punch him right then. It was unconscionable for the censoring officer to do such a thing! But Joe could face a court-martial if he hit him. Joe felt no compliment in being plagiarized; but to respond as he wanted at that moment would have only landed him in the brig. So, he kept his hands busy on the gun he was repairing. But it wasn't easy. And that day he came very close to spending the rest of his military career in jail.

Another case of borderline insubordination was averted only because Joe's commanding officer took his part. The man who had designed the high-tech computer that interfaced with Joe's 90-mm cannon came to Belgium to see his "baby" in action. It was so important to him that he came all the way from Washington, D.C.! This gentleman, uninvited, investigated Joe's private turf, poking his way around this and that. Joe eyed him suspiciously, but kept silent in the face of all that brass dazzling in the afternoon sunshine.

"How long do you keep it going, soldier?" the man asked, nodding in the direction of the computer.

"Twenty-four hours a day," Joe replied.

"Twenty! . . ." the man blustered. "You have to turn it off! You've got to turn it off for ten minutes after every use! Didn't you read the manual?"

"The enemy doesn't read the manual," Joe responded coolly.

"But you've *got* to turn it off!" the computer wizard insisted, angry at the soldier's sarcasm.

Joe walked a few feet from him and started gathering rocks. He placed them at the red-faced commander's feet.

"Then the next time those bombs come flyin' over," Joe said to him, "you throw these rocks at them for the ten-minute rest period you think this thing needs."

"Come with me," the officer ordered through clenched teeth. He had had enough of this soldier's impertinence.

"I want this man busted!" he announced to Joe's captain, after he explained what had just happened. Joe's captain looked at his gunner.

"Did you turn it off?" he asked.

"No, sir," Joe replied.

"Good. I'll help you get some more rocks for this gentleman."

"So you didn't get busted, Daddy Joe?" Joe's daughter-in-law handed him a cup of coffee she had fixed during his account.

Joe's mouth curved upward with a mischievous smile

playing about his lips. "Thank you. No, I didn't. But my drinking was bad and I was having a tough time of it—like a lot of the guys. Then, it happened."

His captivated listener set her own cup on the coffee table. "What happened?"

"I fell in love in Belgium," he said wistfully.

One day, he went on to explain, he was busy working on his cannon on the gun platform. Keeping his eyes on what he was doing, he reached blindly around for a screwdriver, only to have it gently placed in his hand. He looked up and there she was. She was clad in a simple brown coat. A beret topped her curly brown hair. Her eyes were as big and alert as those of an inquisitive kitten. She regarded him with curious interest.

Although Joe didn't speak Flemish and she couldn't speak English, over the course of the next few days he learned that her name was Marie and that she was five years old. It was clear all she had ever known in her life was war. She did not run when the Nazi planes started flying overhead. She leaned tightly against Joe, who always had to make sure she was out of concussion range from the loud, firing cannons.

When there was no cannon fire or enemy aircraft, they would play patty-cake or tag. Joe gave her small gifts of candy in exchange for her trusting smiles and offered friendship. It wasn't long before the American soldier had something other than mail from home or a brewed draft to look forward to; he had the visits of a winsome little girl in a brown coat and jaunty beret to brighten his days.

"So you were head over heels in love," his daughter-in-law interjected.

"Oh, I was!" he declared. "I was crazy about that kid!"

Sometime after Marie had handed Joe the screwdriver on the gun platform, Christmas arrived around the world. Even in the war zone. The German bombing raids dwindled to once a day and the American soldiers found themselves with more time on their hands for other pursuits. They decided to host a Christmas party for the local children. The GIs all chipped in and bought toys, gathered food for a buffet, set up a (rather pitiful) Christmas tree, and even arranged for a visit from Santa Claus. Marie's father brought her to the party, leaving her there after letting Joe know he appreciated his watchful protection of his daughter.

Marie had little interest in Santa, but she loved the sad little Christmas tree. Joe figured she had never seen one before in her short life. The tree was simply decorated with colorful paper chains and strung popcorn. Someone had even managed to find some lights for it! Marie was enchanted! The only thing she seemed to like as well as her friend Joe and the scraggly tree she insisted on standing beside was the gift she received that night: a doll. She clung to her new treasure. Just like she would cling to Joe when it was *not* Christmas and the bombs were exploding around them.

The other memorable thing that occurred at that Christmas party was the healing between the local people and the American soldiers. The Americans saw more than the children to whom they were so drawn. They saw the families from which the children came. They saw the local Flemish people as those who had been ravaged daily by the war in their own backyards. For their part, the local people saw a side of the occupying soldiers they had not seen before either. They were no longer simply the men who came into town to get drunk and make trouble, or the men who unwillingly shared responsibility for the destruction of their hospital. They were men who gave generously and happily to children they did not know, men who had memories of happier times in a country on the other side of the ocean.

"A lot of hostility melted like snow that night," he said, remembering the long-ago Christmas. He recalled something else of that time now.

As the winter months had plodded onward after that Christmas, Joe realized his acquaintance with little Marie did more for him than provide him with refreshing companionship. During a period of rest and relaxation it dawned on him. He never drank when Marie was with him! The demon in the bottle had no power to entice him when this little lady with the shy smiles and spontaneous giggles visited him! Although Joe did not understand it at the time, the Loving Father who fashioned both him and Marie brought Joe a spark of hope in the person of Marie. A solitary little girl had immobilized the tentacles of hopelessness that were pulling him nearer to alcoholism.

"She gave me something to look forward to each day," he said wistfully.

"But you never got to say good-bye to her, did you, Dad?"

Joe couldn't see his daughter-in-law's sympathetic gaze, but he could hear it in her voice.

"Nope. I didn't die in Belgium like I thought I would, but we were evacuated one night without any advance notice. I went on to fight elsewhere, but I never got to see my little Marie again. I've got a picture of her somewheres. . . ," he said, his voice trailing off.

"I remember you showing it to me once. She had just the slightest suggestion of a smile on her face as she stood there in her plain coat and simple beret." His one-person audience got up to return their empty coffee cups to the kitchen.

"Yeah," Joe said, the passport in his hand forgotten. "She was something."

"You know, Dad, God tells us that some of us have entertained angels without realizing it," she said, returning to the living room. "Maybe Marie was your angel!

She came and put a misplaced screwdriver in your hand so you couldn't put a bottle of beer in it!"

Joe looked up at his daughter-by-marriage with a brightness in his dim eyes. "You may be right! I never thought of it that way before! Maybe she was an angel for me!" He chuckled to himself, rising from his chair. "Ain't that something!"

CHAPTER 11

Sunday Afternoon Brunch

Sitting around a table waiting for food in a restaurant can be a fun way to learn about people, especially if the people are over sixty and have learned not to take themselves too seriously. These gentlemen or gentlewomen don't mind telling little-known facts of their personal history. It simply begins to roll off their tongues as easily as butter slides down a mound of steaming blueberry hotcakes. A person can learn a lot about others over brunch, like I said. The only unwritten rule? Open your ears and shut your mouth—unless you're popping in a forkful of those yummy buttered-and-syruped hotcakes.

"You want to know why I married my wife?" Glen asked.

We hadn't asked, but that didn't stop him.

"I married her for the tires on her '34 Lafayette. I had a '41 Chevy and needed tires for it."

Irene, his wife, simply smiled demurely and nodded her head. Glen has been married to her for over forty years now. He's not about to leave her even though those tires are long gone, not to mention the Lafayette or Chevy.

"And you know what else?" he goes on to say.

We don't, but that doesn't stop him either.

"I love my wife more than anyone loves his wife, but twenty-four hours a day, seven days a week is just too much."

That's why Glen, who is seventy-one years old and has had open-heart surgery, an abdominal aortic aneurysm repair, and a colon look-see or two all within the last few years, is still working. He works at his paying job and he works at his nonpaying jobs (elder at his church, usher at his church, kitchen helper at his church, visitor of the sick from his church, etcetera). I remember when Glen was home recuperating from his bypass surgery. I mean, he was *home* recovering from his surgery. Every hour of every day for a few weeks.

"He's going to drive me nuts!" Irene had declared in a small circle of friends. "If he's not out of the house soon, we'll both be crazy!"

"Yep," Glen said, repeating himself. "That's why I married my wife. For those tires. And I love her as much as any man loves his wife, but seven days a week, twenty-four hours a day is just too much." Irene concurs with a nod of her head and a roll of her eyes, but holds her peace. The rest of the food had come anyway. But I wanted to hear the rest of the story. One day soon after our Sunday brunch I got it.

Irene grew up all over the eastern and midwestern continental United States. She lived in Ohio, Washington, D.C., Massachusetts, Virginia, and a few other states besides. Her father was a tool and die maker in the employ of the federal government. As a result, Irene and her family never stayed in one place for long. I understand that's often the way of it when you work for Uncle Sam.

"I don't know," she speculated, "maybe we moved every time the rent was due. . . ." That, of course, remains another possibility. She was young. What did she know of rents and utility bills? Back then Dad and Mom knew all that stuff (or sometimes just Dad). Children had other things to capture their interests and ignite their imaginations.

For Irene it was cutouts kept in a cigar box and prisms. She and her brother would grab a couple of their father's prisms and head for the sunshine. They would have contests to see who could start a fire the fastest with their smuggled prisms. Fortunately or not, their successes were minimal.

"Do you know how long it takes to start a couple freshly plucked leaves burning?" she asked me.

Her most vivid memory of the many places they lived was the six months she and her mother and siblings were with her dad in Panama. He worked on the locks there; the family enjoyed the ocean breezes and sunny days. Although Irene was a traveler by virtue of her father's profession, swimming on Christmas Day was an unforgettable *first* for a wide-eyed thirteen-year-old! In every other place where she had ever lived, winter meant snow or cold rain. Never sunny skies and the backstroke! The real beauty of it was that they didn't have to contend with the fearsome inhabitants and monsters of the deep blue sea. Families of Uncle Sam's employees could enjoy all the amenities usually reserved for the wealthy in Panama in 1940. An adjacent hotel pool, filled with ocean brine, had a large grate that kept out the critters and kept in the refreshing, albeit salty, ocean water. It was a great, very protected swimming area.

Irene's stint in Panama was short-lived. Her father was there a year; she and the rest of the family were there only six months. It was just as well, balmy Christmases or no. Her dad was returned stateside in August 1941. Had it been four months later, he would have been stuck in Panama for a long, long time. And the family's separation would have been much more protracted. War does things like that.

The constant traveling continued for several more years. Finally, when Irene was nineteen, the family was moved back to where her dad started: Toledo, Ohio. Irene was finished with school, but she was single and "in those days if your family moved, you moved." She settled—for what would turn out to be the rest of her life —in northwest Ohio. Gregarious Irene quickly made new friends (it was the pattern of her life, after all), and one evening she and a newfound friend went to a local club. Her friend had grown up in Toledo and one of her former school chums was there that night. That chum was Glen. This was when Irene met Glen. This was also when the proverbial fur hit the fan.

Their first exchange was as original as it was inspiring.

"Where have you been keeping this good-lookin' woman?" Glen asked their mutual friend as she introduced him to Irene.

"Flattery will get you nowhere," Irene retorted with the slightest lift of her nose. No midsized city boy was going to bowl *her* over with one compliment! She'd been around the block (and much of the country) a few times.

It must have gotten him somewhere, however. That was the beginning of Irene's "first serious romance," as she calls it.

"It wasn't his," she interjected drolly to me in her narrative.

Their relationship was anything but smooth sailing. They argued. A lot. About everything and about nothing. The engagement was on. The engagement was off. The wedding was on. The wedding was off. She ordered her wedding gown. She sent it back. They set the wedding date; they canceled the wedding date. Irene made it sound like a malfunctioning engine.

"We were engaged," she said, "and then we were disengaged."

All this nonsense went on for a year and a half. I guess Glen stuck it out because he wanted those tires in the worst way. Even Irene admits his car was considered "hot stuff," no matter it was a few years old. But the arguing and bickering and making up again continued, none of it having anything to do with those cars or their tires. They couldn't get enough of each other, but they got too much of each other. They pined away when apart; they feuded when together. Theirs was a most tumultuous relationship bar none. They finally decided they had had it.

They drove to Indiana and eloped. Just like that. They were going to go to a justice of the peace, as they were called back then, but they couldn't even agree on that. So, they found some little, out-of-the-way church with a pastor to match and he performed the ceremony, such as it was.

"Pastor Sapp was his name," she confided. "We

went back there on our twenty-fifth wedding anniversary. The church was still there, but he wasn't." They don't know if Pastor Sapp left the ministry once he married these two combatants or not. It's one of those mysteries of the past. Pastor Sapp would have rejoiced, had he known it, to hear that midway between the elopement and silver anniversary of these on-again, off-again lovers they met Jesus. But that is another story.

As of April 15, tax day of the year 2000, Glen and Irene will have been married fifty years. (She tells me that tax day in 1950 wasn't in April; it was in March. That got changed sometime later. But that, too, is another story.) Like other couples, Irene and Glen have had their share of sorrows and joys and misunderstandings. And like so many of us, they've had an entire fleet of automobiles—complete with tires—in their many years of marital bliss.

Which reminds me. . .did I mention Glen's occupation? He sells used cars. (I think there's some poetic justice in that.) These cars are seldom Chevrolets and they are never Lafayettes, however. Glen is a Ford man now.

"But why did *you* marry *Glen*?" I asked at the end of Irene's remembrance. She giggled like a new bride and blushed ever so slightly.

"Oh, he was just the sweetest thing! And oh, those blue eyes!"

That just goes to show you. Some reasons for

marrying never change. No matter where you grew up.
No matter what your daddy did to make a living. No matter what kind of tires you've got on your automobile.

CHAPTER 12

I Do Two

Y ou two are going to Scandinavia? Sounds wonderful!" Melody exclaimed. "What's the occasion?"

"We're celebrating our twenty-fifth wedding anniversary this year," replied Cheryl with a smiling glance
to her husband.

"You two don't look old enough to be celebrating
your silver anniversary!" piped in Jennifer.

Melody had invited an assortment of people over for
an informal holiday get-together. They had just come
from church and now they were enjoying hamburgers
that had been grilled to perfection by her husband.

"You're entering what I call the Time of the Mixed
Blessing," interjected Renee. "The babies of the past are
out of the house and the grandkids of the future haven't
yet arrived."

"You did send your youngest off to college this fall,
didn't you?" asked Jennifer. Cheryl nodded in affirmation,

swallowing the last of her hamburger.

"Did you two get married here in town? I think I remember you saying once that you're from Illinois." Renee declined an offered refill for her iced tea from Melody.

"No. We got married in Illinois," Roger answered.

"Actually," Cheryl added, "we got married twice in Illinois. On the same day."

"Whaaat?" asked Renee with a quizzical look. "You've got to tell us about this!"

Between soft drinks and people coming and going for one more celery stick or "just one more cookie," this was the tale of the twice-spoken wedding vows.

Twenty-five years ago a couple of college kids in the state of Illinois decided they had met their match in the best sense of the word. Both had gone away to school. They met on campus and love blossomed like so many lilacs in the early spring. Roger asked Cheryl to marry him, she said "yes," and things were on a fast track to the altar.

Before they could tie the knot, they had to make a trip to the county seat for that piece of paper, which makes the whole marriage thing legal. Roger and Cheryl, though both from Illinois, were not from the same home-town or home church. Cheryl's home church was in the midst of relocation. The wedding would be in the new building. Roger, smart young man that he was, asked his future father-in-law in what county the new church was being built, seeing as that was where he and Cheryl would say "I do." "DuPage County" was the response he got. So, the starry-eyed, betrothed duo set aside a day away from their studies and traveled to Wheaton, Illinois, to get their marriage license.

Driving into Wheaton wasn't a popular pastime, particularly when time was at a premium. The couple were finishing up exams and planning a wedding and making trips home to get everything in order. But a marriage license is a necessary component of the Big Day, so the trek was made in good time. All in all, the bride- and groom-to-be were logging some serious miles on their cars in the prenuptial preparations. Even the new church where they would be married had relocated quite a distance from the old church building. That meant a little more driving and more time set aside for the same. But each felt the other well worth the extra work and preparations for their upcoming wedding, as newlywed wannabes are wont to feel.

Fast forward to the day of the wedding.

It's forty-five minutes and counting. The families are doing all those things families need to do on the Day of the Event. Cheryl was cloistered in a room with her giggling bridesmaids, and getting ready to put on her lovely white gown. Excitement was running high! Roger was doing his best to remain calm, and his dad was doing his best (inadvertently) to make Roger more nervous than he already was.

This was it! This was the day!

The pastor performing the ceremony came up to the groom, beaming a big smile of encouragement at him.

"All ready?" he asked cordially, his hand on the groom's shoulder.

"All ready," was Roger's confident reply.

"Got the ring?"

"Got the ring."

"Cars all decorated?"

"Cars are all decorated." Roger looked at his watch and nervously straightened his tie. *What was this, the third degree?* In less than forty-five minutes he would be marrying his sweetheart and best friend. *Are there any details I'm forgetting?* he wondered.

"Got the license?"

"Got the license." He reached into his pocket and handed it to Cheryl's pastor. There were a couple more things he had to see to and he began walking away.

"Uh, Roger. . ." The minister's tone stopped Roger in his tracks. His next words made him break out in a sweat.

"We've got a problem."

"Problem?"

Had Cheryl backed out? Had someone run into one of the cars? Had his best man lost the ring? Was the license phony?

"This license is for DuPage County," the pastor said quietly.

Well, yes, of course it was! . . .

"This is Cook County. I can't legally marry you and Cheryl here."

It took several seconds for the import of the minister's words to sink in. *Did that mean. . . ?*

"Didn't you ask someone from the church about which county we're in?" the pastor asked. "You can't be legally married here. Not with this license!"

Roger didn't reply. *He had asked someone from the church all right! Had his future father-in-law planned this? Was he secretly hoping Roger wouldn't take away his baby girl? Was this a stall to keep him from marrying his daughter? Had he been trying to be funny?*

Roger wasn't laughing. Neither was the minister. But rather than implicate the guilty party, Roger decided silence was the better part of valor. He admits it wasn't like him to maintain his silence when he'd been backed into a corner like a trapped rodent. He bit his tongue and didn't divulge his flawed source. *What were they going to do?*

"What are we going to do?" he asked aloud to no one in particular.

"I can't marry you two here," the minister repeated. "We're in Cook County now."

It was Saturday. Guests had started to arrive. Cheryl was somewhere in the building getting dressed. Everything was coming down to the wire—everything, that is, except the most important thing. Roger felt his knees getting weak and he wasn't even at the altar yet! County offices weren't open on weekends. He had no idea where the county seat for Cook even was, but he would guess it was in Chicago. *Chicago! It might as well be in Timbuktu!*

"What are we going to do?" he asked, repeating himself. A few seconds of silence hung between him and the pastor.

"Get your folks!" the pastor said suddenly, his voice commanding urgency. "And have your mom get Cheryl. Meet me out back."

In less than ten minutes, five people were scrunched together in the pastor's car, which fairly flew down the road. The groom was in his tuxedo; his parents were in the backseat. The pastor was the Andretti behind the wheel, and Cheryl was the very upset bride-to-be seated between her fiancé and the madcap driver who, to be honest, was *way* over the speed limit in a mad dash to get to DuPage County.

Cheryl, who had not been in on any of the above conversation, had been hastily helped *out* of the dress she had just put on. She had had to quickly dress in someone else's clothes. Her future mother-in-law had come racing into her room, hurriedly telling her something about the marriage license. At any rate, Cheryl wasn't about to wear her wedding gown for the first time anywhere but down the aisle of the church! As guests continued to arrive at the church, the most important members of the wedding party had been unceremoniously whisked away from the church.

The pastor pulled into the first gas station they came to out in the previously serene country setting. He ran into the gas station before the attendant could come out to pump gas for him.

"What county is this?" asked the breathless pastor.

"Du. . ." was all he needed to hear. It was less than thirty minutes until the scheduled wedding—in the wrong county.

He jumped back into the car and faced Cheryl. This gas station, this car, this couple, this minister, and a pair of witnesses were in the right county with the right marriage license for the moment.

"Cheryl, do you take this man to be your lawful, wedded husband?"

Cheryl was not a happy young lady at that moment, but the man she had agreed to marry—and his parents—were sitting right there! What else could she say?

"I do," was her meek, weak reply.

"And do you, Roger, take Cheryl to be your lawful,

wedded wife?" the pastor, hands on the wheel, asked Roger around Cheryl's head.

"I do," he replied.

"I now pronounce you man and wife!" the pastor declared with a jamming of the gearshift and a screeching of tires. They careened out of the gas station at breakneck speed to get back to the church on time.

Less than an hour later, Roger and Cheryl repeated those same vows to each other again. The bride had hastily adorned herself in her gown of white. . .again. The groom was wet with perspiration under his black tuxedo. The two witnesses at the previous *legal* proceedings smiled in shaky relief. The pastor said nothing about wildly chauffeuring the two people before him across two counties.

Thus proceeded the planned marriage of the two young lovers. The announced, planned, *ceremonial* proceedings were only fifteen minutes late getting started. Roger and Cheryl were ceremonially wed as planned in a church in Cook County at the appointed day and time. And Roger and Cheryl were legally married the same day a half hour earlier in a car parked outside a gas station in DuPage County.

"Later the pastor told us," Roger said to their laughing audience, "that he learned the hard way to ask about seeing the marriage license before every wedding ceremony he performed." He looked to his wife of twenty-five years.

"He married another couple some time before us," Cheryl said, picking up the story. "Soon after the wedding, they came to him, clearly upset. 'Pastor,' they said, 'what are we going to do? Our marriage license was issued in the wrong county!' "

"The new groom looked to his bride of fourteen days, whose lower lip had begun to quiver," interjected Roger with a glint in his eye.

" 'We've been living in sin for two weeks!' his wife wailed," Cheryl finished. Her husband shared her secret and winked at his wife while their attentive audience struggled with the humor Roger and Cheryl alone saw in this other couple's plight.

"The newlyweds were both well over seventy!" Roger concluded for her. "They had to get married again for mortal reasons as well as for legal and moral ones!"

"I think the person who coined the phrase 'the best laid plans of mice and men' heard it first from a septuagenarian," added Cheryl with a sympathetic smile for the couple they had never met. "And we are probably the only couple in the world who got married twice on the same day."

"Once in a gas station."

"And once in a church," Cheryl agreed with a nod of her head.

"I don't think my father-in-law realizes to this day that he was the reason why we didn't have the right license!" Roger said, standing to his feet.

"And I suppose you're not about to tell him. . . ," Renee said with a knowing grin.

"You've got that right!"

"I just have one regret," Cheryl said.

"What's that, Cheryl?" asked her hostess.

"When the pastor sold that car, he never asked us if we wanted it for sentimental reasons!"

CHAPTER 13

Honeymoon in a Model T

This was something she had not expected.

Florence felt she had been dragged into this. . .let's see, what did the papers she was given at the door call it? She looked again at the glossy, ten-page magazine she held in her hand. "Classic Car Consortium." That was a mighty fancy name for a bunch of cars and people strewn about a field under the hot Tennessee sun! She followed her husband, Cloden, who seemed as intent in his inspection of all these cars as a teenage boy picking out his first razor. They had been on their way to their daughter's home in Ohio when Cloden had seen the sign and suddenly turned off the interstate.

"Let's stop by and take a look-see," he had said.

So here they were for their "look-see." She sighed and followed him to yet one more buffed-up, slicked-up, and probably priced-up antique car. She didn't remember these cars looking quite this good when they were younger. She didn't think the metal was quite so silver nor the paint quite so lustrous back in the 1920s and 1930s. But what did she know? She had been too busy at the time birthing babies, canning fruit and vegetables, or teaching. My! How did she do all that and more to boot?

"Thank You, Jesus," she said under her breath.

"There it is, Florence! Look!"

She brought her focus and attention back to the present to see Cloden quickly sidling up to a restored Model T Ford. He went around to the driver's side as eager as an excited puppy.

"Look at this!" he exclaimed.

Florence poked her head into the opposite side, letting her hand touch the worn, but in amazingly good condition, seat. She looked across at Cloden, who still stood with twinkling eyes behind his bifocals and a smile of triumph on his face.

"Do you remember?" he asked. "Do you remember our first car?"

For a moment Cloden was not the elderly retiree she was married to; he was the strong, handsome young man who had just proposed marriage to her. Her dawning smile matched his.

"How could I ever forget? And what we undertook in that old Ford! We must have been crazy!" she said with a shake of her head.

"And determined," he said, turning his attention to the steering wheel.

Florence straightened her back and walked leisurely around the automobile. It had been more years ago than she cared to count, but she could remember: she and Cloden and their Model T Ford. . . .

Florence had gone to college to become a teacher. She not only taught school, but she helped run an eighty-eight-acre farm with her husband, who was a full-time school administrator and a full-time farmer. The two of them had livestock, including cows and chickens. They had strawberry fields and peach orchards and sold the produce from both to local markets. They reared three children they loved and taught to love the Jesus who first loved them all.

Florence was a voracious reader. When the television came along, it was for watching the news, not for entertainment, games, or a movie theater production that had been formatted to fit her television screen. She and her husband, Cloden, had done without television for most of their lives. To be honest, it was hard to get hooked on television when you had a number of growing children and work enough for a half dozen people.

She and Cloden were never ones to travel in their early years. Except for being college graduates and educators, they lived lives similar to that of their godly parents. They stayed in the same county where they had grown up. They farmed the land. They sent their kids to public school. They were in church every Sunday, and so were their children. They voted and paid their taxes. They worked hard every day. They stayed at home and served up as much love as hospitality to family and friends alike. With the exception of accelerating changes in travel, communication, and technology, their lives had changed little, as I said, from the life they had known as children on their parents' farms. Cloden and Florence could not be called risk-takers or adventurers.

With one exception. Their honeymoon. It would turn out to be a defining moment in their lives.

Cloden and Florence met and fell in love when they were in college. Cloden completed his undergraduate work. Florence had one year of college yet to complete her education when she and Cloden planned their May 1925 wedding. The announcement of their marriage pleased their parents. Their honeymoon plans were another matter.

Cloden and his bride were going to take a cross-country trip to California (from the heartland of Ohio) for their honeymoon. They were going to take this honeymoon trip in Cloden's "you-can-have-it-in-any-color-as-long-as-it's-black" Model T Ford. Florence and

Cloden's parents were not simply displeased with their children's decision. They were adamantly distressed.

"That is too dangerous a thing to do!" was one of the gentler admonitions the young couple received.

Those who remember Model T Fords know "dangerous" might be a weak adjective. A trip across town— let alone across the country—necessitated a well-prepared, handy driver. The driver of a Model T Ford back in 1925 needed:

Gasoline for the engine. There wasn't a "fill-up station" on almost every corner.

A pump for the tires. The air compressors behind the service station weren't there yet either. (And, as we all know, when they did arrive, they seldom worked anyway.)

Additional tires onboard. Those skinny little black balloon things around the wheels were not at all hardy.

The American landscape wasn't exactly replete with our present-day service station–convenience stores and rest stops in 1925. Our expansive network of interstate highways was little more than a figment of someone's imagination. Going from Ohio to California was sure to net the traveler more than his share of unpaved roads. The roads back in the Roaring Twenties were not accommodating to those spindly black balloons. If there even *was* a road.

Motel accommodations? Hotel accommodations? Campground accommodations?

Well, the lack of hotels was no problem. . .as long as one was in a city, which, for most of this trip, Cloden and Florence were not. Motels weren't around yet to *be* a problem. And as far as campgrounds go, it's true that in 1925 some Americans still lived in camps. On the ground. Some had made it to cabins, but not all. In other words, "campgrounds" had not become a popular vacation place to honeymoon or "get away from it all." Not by any stretch of the imagination. But none of this was a problem for Cloden and Florence.

The bride- and groom-to-be were triumphant in their revelation: They planned to tent camp all the way to the Golden State! Others might have to do the tent thing out of necessity; they would do it out of a sense of adventure! They were going to have time with each other and with the great continental American landscape on a big scale! Convention be hanged! It was time to break out of their protective Ohio shell and see the sights! All the protests and warnings fell on deaf ears. These two adults, aged twenty-four and twenty, had made up their minds. They were getting married. They were going to California. They were going to see the country—when they weren't changing tires or trying to navigate around road holes big enough to swallow their Model T Ford whole.

They packed their clothes. They packed food. They packed cooking utensils. They would be preparing and eating most of their meals "on the road." They packed bedding and a tent for those cold nights under the stars. They took gasoline. And containers for more. They took water. And containers for more. Maps, such as they were. Tires and more tires. A pump and tools to keep the Ford going when it no longer wanted to keep going. And an ax for safety and for chopping wood to build cooking fires. Sounds like a vacation. . . ?

It was a memorable trip. They did make it—in that black Model T Ford—from Ohio to California and back again in the summer of 1925.

I have no idea how.

They ran into some nasty weather during their trek. Major nasty weather. In their marital bliss, it was probably the one thing for which they had not planned. But they made do, as only starry-eyed newlyweds can. It wasn't unusual to have to stop every hour or two to pump or repair a tire. Or *tires.* There were incredibly long stretches of road (I use the term loosely) where Florence and Cloden saw no civilization. None. If they wanted time alone and together, they certainly found it. In abundance. But there was one other incident on which they had not planned. And this one was far and above worse than the bad weather.

It *was* dangerous, as their parents had warned them. It could have proven deadly.

Cloden and Florence had stopped for the night in the middle of nowhere, which was something they did quite frequently once they got past Illinois. They found the perfect spot for their overnight stay: a secluded, quiet, beautiful location near a fresh-flowing stream that would meet their needs for washing up and cooking. They had had their final meal of the day and everything was then put away for the night. Tired from the long hours in the automobile, they were happily tucked in for the evening.

It was as dark as dark could be. No flashlight was in hand and no campfire or candles burned. No friendly moon was out to illumine crack and crevice. As Milton so succinctly put it, it was "darkness visible." It was a night to quickly lure one to a soundless sleep. Nothing but crickets or the croaking of frogs near the water interrupted the soothing silence.

Suddenly, the hypnotizing night sounds were broken. By human voices. Sinister, menacing, conspiring human voices. The speakers, confident no one was around to hear them, unhesitatingly conferred with one another. As their voices drifted across the gentle waters of the bubbling stream, Cloden and Florence were immediately alert and frightened. The speakers were planning a bank robbery.

Florence reached for Cloden's hand. Her heart was beating wildly. Her breathing almost matched the erratic pace of her heart. Would the robbers hear her pounding heart or frightened breathing? She was certain Cloden could hear it!

For his part, Cloden reached for his ax with his free hand. He hadn't planned on using it for anything other than firewood! But neither had he planned to be miles from Anywhere with his frightened young bride, over-hearing the plans of base men. The minutes grew long and tense. Cloden was ready to fight for and protect his wife. Florence began that at which she was to become so proficient—simple, straightforward prayer in simple, straightforward trust. As she and her new husband sat huddled in their tent, she prayed away discovery.

Ever so gradually and quietly, the voices faded into the night. Unmindful that they were less than a stone's throw from a bounty of supplies, cash, food, and a means of rapid travel, the thieves made their way farther up the stream and away from the trembling, thankful twosome. As their footsteps died away, the sound of crickets and frogs once again punctuated the wilderness silence.

Cloden and Florence were safe! Their moment of terror and danger had passed. In the morning there was no sign anyone else had ever been in the area of the couple's almost-shattered place of repose. There were no cell phones to call and warn authorities. As long as they traveled through Colorado on their way to California, Cloden and Florence never heard of a bank robbery there—even after they once again came in sight of civilization! That their experience was real, they never doubted. But what came of the plans of evil men they had come so close to confronting, the young couple never knew. They continued on their way to California. Cloden and Florence returned to Ohio as planned by the time the school year was ready to begin again. They had accomplished what they set out to do in their trusty Model T Ford!

"It was quite a honeymoon trip!" Florence said, coming back to the present. "I liked our 'Silver Bullet'—that travel trailer we had back in the '70s—best of all. Sink, beds, air-conditioning—that was traveling!"

"Yes, we had enough of adventure and danger to last us for a while after our honeymoon, didn't we?" Cloden replied, chuckling in agreement. The two of them walked away from the car that was much smaller than they had remembered it.

"Give me campgrounds with showers—and roadside rest stops with flush toilets—any day of the week!" she said.

"And a sedan with a cell phone!" Cloden exclaimed.

They paused to look back one more time at the displayed Model T Ford. They shook their heads, shared a smile, and left the Classic Car Consortium holding hands. And for a moment. . .not looking all that different from the honeymooners they were in 1925!

CHAPTER 14

Prayer Warrior

Prayer warriors are a rare breed. They are those unique individuals who take to heart those heady words of the prophet, Samuel, when he said, "Far be it from me that I should sin against the Lord by failing to pray for you" (1 Samuel 12:23 NIV). These dear saints well know that failure to uphold others in prayer is more an affront to God than an injury to those to whom we've said "I'll pray for you" and didn't.

When someone has a need at our church, Harold is the prayer warrior who's sought. Harold does not stand out in a crowd. His back is bent; he's neither as tall nor as straight as he once was. He has glasses to help him see, hearing aids to help him hear, and a cane to help him walk. He doesn't get out much anymore, particularly after dark. He's dispensed with driving; he has a young sidekick in his late sixties to help him get out and about. Long ago Harold's children grew up and moved out. His wife left him some years ago for the Better Life, where she no longer lives her days beneath the underside of the clouds. Harold had to give his trusty canoe of more than fifty years to one of his sons. It got to be too much to carry into and out of the water, though he had done it effortlessly for years. When he was eighty-five he sold his house and moved into a small apartment. But the one unchanging thing in all these changes is Harold's walk with God. The King James Version of the Bible would call it his "conversation" with God. That has not altered, except for the better.

Harold was one of those souls blessed to grow up in a home where God was revered and Jesus was the "unseen Guest at every meal." His family lived in a farming community and attended a small town church. Harold was ten years old when he went to work. His father had died and he and his mother moved to the city. There were mouths to feed and bills to pay. Perhaps it was back then that Harold began learning his lessons on prayer. Or maybe it was in the years he and his wife poured their energies and resources into child evangelism. Either way, Harold became a man of prayer. As he has been given more time to spend in prayer and less time to spend otherwise, Harold has made prayer the "first work," as Oswald Chambers called it.

When you ask Harold to pray, he prays. Not as soon as he gets home or when he has his quiet time. He pulls you into the Holy Place—whether it's in the church sanctuary or the church parking lot—right then and there. Harold doesn't mess around when asked to pray.

In the past, pastors were hard-pressed to beat Harold to the hospital to pray with someone. When the pastor did happen to arrive before Harold, those visits turned into prayer meetings once Harold arrived. He never hesitated to draw in anyone else in the immediate vicinity, be it another visitor, a patient, or a caregiver. A bit of heaven was coming down, so you'd better be ready to be in on it! And Harold made no shy apologies for doing what God has instructed all His children to do. These days Harold attends hospital room prayer meetings by proxy. He's unable to get out as readily as he once was. But the lack of mobility is no deterrent to this prayer warrior! He's praying at home just as earnestly as he once did at hundreds of hospital beds. He needs neither automobile nor chauffeur to get his prayers to the right place.

When Harold was a young man of eighty-two or so and still living in his small house, he spent many hours praying for the salvation of his neighbors. He didn't know how many, if any, of them had received God's gift of eternal life and had committed themselves fully to Jesus Christ. This weighed heavily on Harold, especially when he prayed. So it was time to find out. He hit the streets praying. And smiling.

He would knock on a door, introduce himself, and say in his firm, yet inoffensive way, "We're doing a survey to find out about people's religious interests. Do you have a few minutes?"

If the person did not, Harold thanked him or her and went on his way. He sent his prayers for them heavenward; he started his feet moving earthward to the next neighbor. If the neighbor did have a few minutes, Harold would gently tell him about Jesus and what it takes to enter into a relationship with Him. Then he would offer to pray with him.

"Who was the 'we' you were doing the survey with, Harold?" someone once asked him.

"The Lord and I!" he replied with a smile. "The Lord wanted me to do this, so I did. If anyone ever asked me, 'Who's we?' I'd tell them. But nobody ever asked and I was just doing what I was told to do. The Lord said, 'Do it,' so I did. Praise the Lord." (Harold begins and ends almost every conversation with "Praise the Lord.")

Harold is a seasoned prayer warrior. As he grows older, he grows bolder. When he moved into his apartment building, he did the same thing that he had previously done in his neighborhood. Well. . .almost the same thing. He dropped the fluff. A gentle knock at the door still announced his arrival and he still accepted a dismissal as graciously as ever. But he became as direct in his approach to people as he is in his prayers to God.

He didn't always meet with success, but that neither discouraged him nor stopped him. He knew he had a message and knew he might be his neighbors' only messenger. Discouragement and defeat are not in Harold's vocabulary, no matter that few may heed his counsel.

"I'm still working on them," he recently told me, a twinkle in his eyes. "One of my neighbors has cancer. You know, I had cancer and I can talk to people who have cancer. The doctor told me in 1986 I had three months to live."

Apparently this doctor's prognosis was what the medical community calls a "second opinion." God's opinion was the first and differed somewhat from that of Harold's doctor. As I type this it's 1999 and Harold turns ninety years young next week.

But as I said, this soldier of the cross has dispensed with the fluff. Harold's deep love for his Savior and his genuine concern for others are what make him the prayer warrior that he is. It's etched in every line of his face, it sparkles in his eyes, and it's laced throughout his every conversation.

"Have you got a few minutes?" he'll ask. "I'd like to talk with you about Jesus. Then we can pray."

CHAPTER 15
The Cat's Meow

Dogs, cats, cows. . .you name it, we had it. Some were pets, some were strays, some were raised for slaughter. I was surrounded by animals from the time the dog could walk up to me and lick my face uninvited!" Leanne paused in her remembrance. "I think my first word was 'moo' instead of 'mama' or 'dada.' "

Leanne grew up on a farm. She is a petite, soft-spoken lady married to a pastor who has more energy in his little finger than most of us have in our entire bodies. Leanne has no trouble keeping up with his contagious enthusiasm. They're both "city slickers" now, but that has in no way dimmed Leanne's memories of growing up on her family's Canadian beef farm. If anything, life away from the farm has probably sharpened those recollections.

Leanne has wonderful memories from her childhood in Canada that did not include all the glitz or entrapments of city life. Long days in the barn, carefree walks through the meadow down to the stream— amusements many city dwellers would no doubt find as boring as the panoramic two-hours-long musicals of the early 1960s.

One might surmise that the life of a domestic or farm animal in such an idyllic setting would be, well, the cat's meow. Think of it. Hay or straw brimming with mice and micelettes for even the most discerning barn cat's palate. Acre upon acre of open field for pooch to run, bark, sniff, and explore with never a worry about a "SHUT UP, YOU MANGEY MUTT!" being shrieked at him or, worse yet, a poisoned pork chop to silence forever his madcap misadventures. No demands on the cows either; grass to chew to their hearts' content and a fresh supply of cool, running water. No need to even dirty a glass— or, in her case, a bucket—for a good slurp of that farm fresh, gurgling brook H_2O.

Doesn't it all sound lovely? Even if you are a diehard city slicker, you must admit a day at Leanne's Canadian homestead sounds deliciously relaxing and soothing. Quiet. Calm. Peaceful. And it was.

Most of the time.

But we're living "this side of the Fall," which is a preacher's fancy way of saying even big, beautiful, Canadian beef farms are not paradise. The farm where Leanne grew up is a case in point. At least it was if you were one of the animals who called Leanne's childhood Canadian beef farm "home."

"What you call cattle ranches here in the U.S.A.," she says in her soft-spoken manner, "we call beef farms. We raised cows for slaughter and not for milk. But you know, I never forged what you might call lifelong friendships with any of our animals."

"That's because none of them lived very long!" her husband interjects. The two of them snicker about their private family joke, and with little coaxing Leanne talks of her childhood. . . .

"With the cows being raised for slaughter, we kids had no close ties with any 'Bossy' or 'Elsie.' The bull calves were going to be steers and the steers were going to be steak, burgers, or chuck roasts. We weren't about to make friends with somebody's supper!"

"But sometimes the cow's untimely demise came sooner than expected!" her husband adds.

"One of our calvers was a case in point," she says.

"I never was a country boy myself—grew up mostly in the U.S. and a bit in Africa. But I always thought the bovine mentality was such that cows knew enough to come in out of the rain when the barometer is dropping like a rock out of a three-story window!"

"Not this calver!" Leanne continues with a laugh. "One day the wind started blowing, the billowing black clouds rolled in, and the rains came down diagonally! I remember it became as dark as night in the middle of the day! The lightning would illuminate the twigs of the tree outside my room. I could hear the 'flick, flick, flick' of the small branches beating against the windowpane! At least, I could hear that sound when the crashing thunder wasn't shaking loose every shingle on the house!"

"It was weather fit for neither man nor beast!" her husband interjects with a dramatic wave of his arm.

"You'd think she would have enough sense to come in out of the rain!" Leanne says as much to her husband as to her audience of interested listeners.

"You'd think that, yes."

"But she didn't."

"No, she didn't," he repeats for effect.

"She moseyed down to the stream to stand obliviously and blissfully next to the single tree there. I'm sure that tree was losing as many branches in the storm as leaves in the fall!" Leanne fans out her arms, mimicking the furiously waving branches of the solitary tree. "The storm ranted and raged, but this cow leisurely helped herself to the thick, well-moistened grass that, like a siren's song, temptingly beckoned her to be heedless of the wind and rain!"

"Life was good! The grass was green! The water was blue!" her husband adds with a flare. And then, as an afterthought: "And she wasn't heavy with calf."

"Best of all!" Leanne says in agreement, rolling her eyes. She pauses for effect. "Then, it happened! Raindrops the size of golf balls came down from the heavens, pummeling plant and puddle!"

"Leaves and loose twigs, wind-ripped from the tree, danced through the air in wild disarray!"

"Suddenly. . .the air was charged with electricity! Literally," Leanne says with finality.

"Fortunately," her husband says in a droll tone, "the lightning bolt missed the solitary oak. Not so fortunately. . ." He turned an uplifted hand to his wife.

"It did not miss the Black Angus standing *next* to the tree. Zap! Our Black Angus became instant char-grilled burger. She was a very well done crispy critter." Leanne scrunched up her face.

"Blackened remains were all that was left of this bovine beastie," her husband commented.

"How sad!" From one of the listeners in the small gathering.

"Well. . .yes and no. Maybe she was doomed from the beginning. Did I remember to tell you her name?" Leanne asks, well knowing she did not.

"I suppose it was 'Lightning.' " This retort from one of the males in the group.

"Close, but no." Leanne flashes her partner in the tale a satisfied smile. "Should we tell them?"

"By all means! Tell them what your poor flash-fried cow's name was before her untimely demise."

"Blackie."

CHAPTER 16
Lessons Learned

California brings to mind the word BIG: big state, big trees, big mountains, big coastline, big cities, big traffic jams, big taxes. Size is not everything, however, and it's in some of the small things where the best is not necessarily big. Grant grew up in this big state and traveled occasionally to a place near a big marine corps base named Twenty-nine Palms. This story comes from California, but it is not about the Big Coastline State or Twenty-nine Palms. It's more about Grant and what he saw and thought during and after a rock hunt. And a little about Grant's mother, too.

Grant had an eye for simple beauty and the not so simple reflections that sometimes accompany a person's appreciation of simplicity. Grant often put his thoughts eloquently on paper. His ability to do so came naturally from his mother and supernaturally from the Father who made them both.

Grant's mother was a unique woman. She taught grades one through six in a sod hut in Kansas. It was possible to teach children with an assortment of ages and maturity levels back then. All at once. In the same place.

School was where you went to add to the instruction you first received at home. If you did not do as the teacher instructed, you not only had to deal with the consequences of it at school, you had to deal with the consequences at home. Parents didn't sue teachers back then; adults stuck together. If you got into trouble at school, you were generally in *more* trouble when you got home! Spankings were a common means of correction back then. If you got a spanking at school, you got another one when you got home.

No questions asked. If the teacher told your parents you had not conducted yourself properly during recess, your parents didn't question her observation. If the teacher said your conduct was inappropriate, your conduct was inappropriate. A child's parents didn't think the teacher was trying to stifle your creativity or infringe on your rights. And they certainly didn't "get on the horn" to talk to their attorney! But that was then.

Grant's mother did not drive to school in a sport utility vehicle the size of a tank. Nor did she need a real army tank to get her safely to and from the sod hut. This teacher rode a horse. Mounted up with bag and baggage, she did her duty by her students five days a week, good weather or bad. When she married and moved to California, Grant's mother changed hats and became a businesswoman. She rented a huge packing house, hired as many as a dozen other women, and put up dried fruit and nut packs from the fruit farm her husband owned.

Another move to Hollywood dictated one more career change for the talented lady whom Grant called "Mother." There she left off her previous equestrian travels and taught elocution to Hollywood hopefuls. If you were an up-and-coming star or starlet (even if only in your imagination), you had better know how to express yourself: properly, succinctly, eloquently. This teacher and elocutionist made sure you did! And when she wasn't doing that, she took part in early movies as one of the sea of faces seen in group or mob scenes!

With such a colorful childhood, Grant grew up well able to express what pleased him, certainly hoping his observations would nurture in others the wonder of life he enjoyed. Fortunately for those who came after Grant —and long after his mother—he wrote down some of his observations.

Back in the 1960s Grant and his wife often went rock hunting. On one of these day trips, the two of them came upon a "single, lonely grave set upon the east bank of a rocky wash," as he phrased it. This grave site was not in a well-kept cemetery; it was at the Old Dale mining area. Apparently, no loved ones or relatives of the one beneath the monument went there to reflect on the transience of life. The gravestone jutted heavenward in cheerless solitude. Grant described it this way:

> *Here, beside a cairn of darkened, desert varnished rocks, a small gray monument stands erect after half a century of exposure to the relentless elements. The carving upon its face is beginning to show the ravages of time: sharp edges softened, the simple legend imperceptibly dimmed. . . . The years 1903–1904 and the simple word "Baby" inscribed here can no longer be easily discerned.*

For a long time the two of them, Grant and his wife, stood there wondering about the unnamed life that had been. A half century of time had muted what more they might have discovered there in the midst of the desert flowers. Years later when they decided to visit the site again, they found that others had not been so moved to silent reflection. The grave had been vandalized; what was left in the wake of the destruction no longer gave passers-by leave of the present to ponder the past or the future.

Fortunately, not all things of worth can be vandalized. Grant and his wife had years to consider what, for them, had been an added lesson from the simple gravestone. In the same account as recorded above, before the final, disappointing return to the solitary little grave, Grant had concluded:

> *One is naturally led to think of another child born in a harsh desert land much like this. A child destined to change the world, to bring a new concept to man of religion and His involvement with it. His name hangs brightly against the backdrop of history and shines as brightly within the hearts of many of us. A Child whose coming was heralded by a great star shining overhead and who was welcomed by Magi bearing gifts. By contrast, this babe came and went unnoticed and unsung, almost unmarked. Still, when the night wind mourns softly across the slope, the desert stars keep vigil here and in the spring of the year, a great star stands forth in the eastern sky, promising a new day and a better world in which to live.*

Vandals had wantonly destroyed what the elements more slowly and without rancor had begun to ruin. But neither the elements nor vandals (nor sitting in a sod hut schoolhouse) can destroy all of the richest lessons of life. The true treasures remain untouched and untouchable.

Grant said it when he stood at the grave site of a child and wrote about the promised "new day and better world." Jesus Christ said it this way:

> *"But store up for yourselves treasures in heaven, where moth and rust do not destroy, and where thieves do not break in and steal. For where your treasure is, there your heart will be also."*
>
> (MATTHEW 6:20–21 NIV)

Words and lessons worth pondering.

CHAPTER 17
Slap in Two

Just when you think you've mastered the English tongue, including the American vernacular, you hear something that sets your teeth on edge, tickles your proverbial funny bone, or makes absolutely no sense at all. For those of you outside of the Midwest, let me give you an example of what we in the Midwest take for granted every day, yet people from parts elsewhere in the country think bizarre at best and nonsense at worst.

"Pop" for us is not usually a person nor is it a term of pugilism. Pop for a Midwesterner is something that comes in an aluminum can or in a two-liter bottle and goes by well-known brand names. When our friends Walt and Sarah moved here from New Jersey, they were appalled to hear "soda" referred to in such a cryptic way. Of course, when they ask in a restaurant, "What kind of soda do you have?" any waiter or waitress under thirty looks at them as if they just flew in from another planet. . . . I suppose coming from New Jersey would be considered by some as being from another planet.

It's interesting how "soda pop" became "soda" or "pop" depending on where you live. We forget, and most younger folks probably don't even know, that not so long ago a "soda" was a drink that was often served with ice cream. Like a root beer float. (Not that the root beer floats; the ice cream floats on the root beer once you prod it enough to make a proper mess.) Anyway, you bought sodas at a soda fountain or soda shop and those delicious treats were made by soda jerks. Call somebody a "soda jerk" now and watch out!

My friend Jo grew up on a big dairy farm in Wisconsin. A BIG dairy farm. She and her sisters shared a language not unlike good old American English. It was dissimilar enough from the original, however, to leave some of us scratching our heads and running to find our 1963 *Funk and Wagnall's Standard College Dictionary* when these fair-haired siblings got together to chat in their unique Dairy-land Dialect. In retrospect I would have to say it wasn't their words that were so difficult, but the lack of them. These sisters talked in syllables or phrases. A few examples are in order. . . .

"Are you sear?" Jo replied breathlessly after her younger sister made a pointed comment about a local news event. Overhearing this conversation, thinking I'm getting the hang of this secret code of theirs, I thought: *She must mean "sincere."*

Wrong. "Sear" is short for "serious."

Then there was "crisslaunchwise." If I understand it correctly, crisslaunchwise means something akin to diagonally. The first time Jo's husband-to-be heard it, he did a double take.

"Criss*what*?" he asked, laughing.

"Crisslaunchwise!" Jo gave him a look that said: *DON'T tell me you've never heard this!*

"*What* is 'crisslaunchwise'?" His syllables came out between chuckles that were bordering on guffaws.

"You know," she said, motioning with her hands, "like sideways or angled."

"Diagonally?" he asked.

"Not exactly. . . ," she said slowly, but then put her hands on her hips. A pose of challenge. "You've never heard 'crisslaunchwise'?" she asked, skeptical of his purported ignorance. (But perhaps she was a little less sure of herself. Thus the pose.)

"Of course not!" he retorted. No halfhearted attempts covered up his laughter now. "It's not a word!"

"It is so! It's in the dictionary!" (This from a college sophomore.) She was rankled now. Her blue eyes flashed in ready defense.

It had not been in any dictionary her boyfriend had ever seen. Or anyone else has ever seen for that matter. He challenged her and they worked their way through a number of dictionaries. I need not tell you who was right.

And who was in error.

You'll find "crosswise" and "crossways" and "criss-cross" and "cross-purposes" in the dictionary. But no "crisslaunchwise." Maybe the "term" was coined when some novice sailor launched his craft "crisscrosswise"— and then expressed himself to the harbor patrol with language skills matched only by his seamanship.

Here's another—and I've heard people use it who grew up nowhere in the Midwest, including on any big Wisconsin dairy farm.

"Do you want to go with?"

That's it: "Do you want to go with?"

That's what some say—people who are educated and for whom English is their mother tongue.

"Do you want to go with."

With WHAT? With WHOM?

Don't these people know that "with" is a preposition and therefore it must have an object? Don't they know it's improper English to end a sentence with a preposition? Even if you're not a fan of semantics or grammar, doesn't ending a question with "with" set like a drill bit powering its way into your rotted molar? As we used to say when I was a kid, it gives me the heebie-jeebies just to think about it. It's right up there (or down there) with "libary" and "warshing the clothes."

Okay, sometimes it *is* proper to use a preposition at the end of a sentence.

She needs tools to work with.
What's this made of? What is it good for?
What are you talking about?

As a product of the Midwest, or American culture for that matter, I am guilty of at least one unusual use of an American colloquialism. I have used "the fifth degree" in my writing when I meant "the third degree" (an interrogation or intense questioning). You "take the fifth" when you invoke your Fifth Amendment right to refuse to answer questions. Since one might precipitate the need for the other, well, you can see how they might get misused.

It only gets worse if you go from one (supposedly) English-speaking country to another. A couple we know went to Australia as missionaries some years back. They had no need to attend language school; they were, after all, only going Down Under, where most of the people already spoke English.

. . .Not any English they'd ever heard. A "body shop" is not the same thing to an Aussie as it is to an American. (I won't say anything beyond its *not* being a place to take your banged-up car.) And "chips" are not those crunchy things you eat out of a bag. But I'm getting carried away. . . .

At any rate, moving around from place to place should improve your listening skills, if nothing else. You really need to pay attention to follow the gist of some conversations.

Not long ago I was privy to a conversation between my mother and an elderly Floridian who was not transplanted from the Midwest or anywhere else. Henry was born and reared in Florida and, when his time comes to exit the confines of time, I'm sure he'll make his exit from the state where he's lived his entire life. This gentleman has a southern accent and the regional expressions that go with it to make Robert E. Lee roll over in his grave and stand up proud. I was sure my mother was following little of Henry's tale of his open-heart surgery. (You know how all folks who have had open-heart surgery love to swap stories after the fact. Henry is no exception.) He had come by to see how my dad, who had just had bypass surgery himself, was faring.

While Henry was on the subject of medical procedures, he digressed somewhat from open-heart surgery. One minute he was telling how "the meat on both sides of [his] breastbone was turribul sore" after they had given him "those six-hundred volts." The next minute he was talking about some back surgery he had had. Somehow the memory of those "six-hundred volts" catapulted him into sharing about a previous back injury. Frankly, I missed the beginning of the back injury tale as I struggled with this strange vision of Henry looking like some kind of chicken part being zapped like Blackie the Cow.

"Yep," he said, "I broke my back slap in two. Broke it slap in two."

Again, I began to ponder the possibilities. Now I've heard of "slap-dab," which means "directly," and even "smack-dab," which means "exactly" or "squarely." And, of course, a "slapstick" is a stage prop (two flat pieces of wood bound at one end) that makes that onstage slap sound realistic. Perhaps one day a slapstick broke smack-dab in two and a colloquialism was born. Hmm.

Nevertheless, how a man pushing eighty could have broken his back "slap in two" and can still get around like someone half his age is something I cannot fathom. Henry walks, drives, bikes, and goes where and when he wants as easily as the fittest of Florida's snowbird population. He either had an orthopedic surgeon the likes of which the world has never seen, or he has an uncommon gift for painting graphic word pictures with his unique, regional command of the English language.

I like to think Henry is like those Wisconsin dairy farm girls: just saying what they mean and meaning what they say. Or simply saying what they mean the way *they* mean to say it. Whether or not any of the rest of us knows what's being said is inconsequential to the colorful rendition of the tale.

CHAPTER 18

When the Wall
Came Down

For the first time in over a generation, people could come and people could go.

The wall was down!

The Union of Soviet Socialist Republics was gone. Maps and globes had to be redone; countries whose names had been muted under the banner of USSR were declaring themselves very much alive and very much their own. Even cities took on their former names. Leningrad was Saint Petersburg once again. What many had prayed for, had suffered for—had died for—had become a reality! Freedom had returned to the land east of Europe! Religious freedom had returned to those who for years had been told and taught: "There is no God."

The wall separating East from West was a barrier no longer. People eagerly exited; other people even more eagerly entered.

Carmen and her husband, Gunther, were far from the wall when it came down. They were living in the perpetual heat and humidity of Indonesia, where they had lived since 1961. She was a young wife of twenty-three with a toddler when the three of them stepped off their slow-moving ship and onto Indonesian soil for the first time. (American missionaries arriving in distant lands weren't jumping on or off jetliners back then!) For thirty-two years they helped establish Christian churches in this nation of thousands of islands, initially starting in Kalimantan/Borneo. They ate and loved the spicy foods and exotic fruits of Indonesia, sampling most, if not all, of the two hundred-plus varieties of bananas grown in this nation of islands. They reared their children there, which meant sending them off to boarding school in another country.

Carmen and Gunther grew used to the steamy weather and, as modernization invaded their tropical paradise, they grew to tolerate the heavy smog of the exploding capital city of Jakarta. They had little doubt they would live in Indonesia until they retired. To Indonesia God had brought them; in Indonesia they would remain until retirement.

Unknown to them, God had other plans. And His plans didn't as yet include their retirement.

Carmen said it this way in a letter dated June 1993: *"God is calling us to Russia. . .[I] can't quite believe this is for real yet."* A few sentences later she added that whatever awaited them there in Russia, she was sure it wouldn't be *"as nice as Indonesia—even though they eat RATS up in Menado. . . . It's a specialty."* Less than a year later they traded in their sunglasses and swimming suits for the heaviest, warmest winter coats they could get their hands on. They pitched their sandals and invested in some serious snow boots. They exchanged their familiar Indonesian for the eternal language of Russian. (Another missionary to Russia quipped that he was sure Russian is the language of heaven. It takes forever to learn it!)

Carmen was in her fifties when she and Gunther, who was sixty, arrived in Volgograd, Russia, in January 1994. Their church mission board decided that language school was not an option for them because they would be leading the mission team and there would be no time. It was assumed that since both Carmen and her husband had been born in Germany, they would be able to communicate well enough with the German-speaking peoples who at one time settled the region of Volgograd. So they were told. Well, there is misinformation and there is misinformation. This was *misinformation.* They found no

one who admitted speaking German. No one who spoke
any Indonesian. And not many spoke English, as you
might guess. But God had directed them; God would
handle the language barriers. And, amazingly, He did.

Carmen's first letters to friends this side of the
Atlantic were written in her beautiful script. Her type-
writer was unusable until the right electrical outlet
transformer could be found. She equated finding such
a transformer to finding the proverbial needle in a hay-
stack. Computers? Please! This was 1994! Computer
availability—especially to pioneering missionaries in
Russia —was a ways off yet. A long ways off. So, what
were Carmen's first impressions as she and Gunther
"started over" in Volgograd? Let her tell you. . . .

> There is so much that totally blows our minds of
> what was put in our minds about this country
> and what and how things are in actuality.
> Definitely this country and people are more closely
> linked with the Asian way of doing things than
> the European or Western mind-set. There have
> actually been times in the market here when I
> caught myself thinking I was in Asia, only to be
> totally startled to look up into, what we think,
> [are] European faces. Gunther and I keep saying
> to ourselves this, the economy, the stores, the situa-
> tion is so much like Indonesia was in 1961 when

we first arrived there. This truly is a country time forgot. Praise God, He did not forget. . .Russians are like sponges right now, soaking up and feeding their starved souls. . . . Every single person in this country (aside from the leaders, but even they, I believe) has a story to tell of fear, persecution, and terrible hardship. The people are so open, their faith so childlike as they reach out to God, whom they know nothing about. Then as they see God working in their lives and see answers to prayers, they nearly explode with joy. They throw their arms around us and thank us over and over for coming to tell them about Jesus.

The rest of Carmen's letter—and subsequent letters —abounded with this same joy and enthusiasm. What is not apparent in these words is what God had started doing and was doing in Carmen's own heart and life at this time. You see, Carmen did not grow up loving Russian people. She did not even like them. Some might say she despised them. Quite frankly, she had no use for them at all one way or the other. A seed of indifference for Russians had been planted in Carmen's heart long before she came to Russia. Long before she had even stepped on Indonesian soil. She had scarcely given it a thought in all those years. God had given her long-buried prejudice some thought, however, and was about to confront this daughter of the Light with the necessity of tearing down some walls of her own.

Carmen grew up in a happy home in East Germany. She and her three siblings had a "fun and very comfortable life" growing up, as she puts it. Her dad, an owner of a large electronic store, was considered a wealthy man in their hometown. Summers were spent at the ocean in their summer home. One of Carmen's most cherished memories of their life in Germany was the last time her extended family was all together.

One of Carmen's cousins was getting married. Everyone in the family gathered at an uncle's farm for three days of merriment, eating, and celebration. For this young German girl who was used to life in the city, it was an exciting time of adventure during the day and sleeping with her cousins in the hayloft at night. And the food! Pantry shelves were piled high with cakes and desserts of every variety; Carmen called it "mountains of food." They did not have ice cream, but they ate pure whipped cream until their coronary arteries screamed for relief. But their protected, close life as a family came to an abrupt end in 1944, less than a year after this three-day wedding celebration. The Russian army marched into Germany.

Carmen was seven years old when the Russian soldiers invaded her homeland. She and her family had to flee for their lives. Packed in a train with other refugees, they traveled south through Germany, staying briefly in the region of the Black Forest. Eventually they fled to Austria, but all this was without her father. Unknown to her and her family, he had been captured by Russian soldiers and was held as a prisoner of war.

Carmen and her family were without their father for almost two years. Their mother was forced to provide them with their daily needs. Life was no longer idyllic. Summers at the ocean had become a thing of a distant past. Carmen's mother did sewing for the farmers around them to provide for her family. Lothar and Regina, Carmen's older brother and sister, also helped provide for the family by working for the farmer next door. Payment was in vegetables, fruit, and occasionally meat.

The war finally came to an end, but their family's days of separation did not. Carmen's father began his trek to be reunited with his family, but he was recaptured in Russian territory and once again imprisoned, no matter that the war was "officially" over. When he was finally released in 1947, it was because his failing health made him a liability to those who had "detained" him. Fearful of being recaptured or shot, Carmen's father traveled at night until he was reunited with his family. In the months of his long recovery with his family in Austria, Carmen's father repaired watches and clocks, a trade he had learned as a child himself. In a final escape from the horror that had come with the

Russian forces and the changed borders of post WWII
Germany, in 1952 fourteen-year-old Carmen and her
family immigrated to America. Yet like others who have
grown up or lived in a war zone, young Carmen had
already developed some strong opinions and prejudices.
War often does that to people.

Carmen had learned to distrust Russia and its people.
They had taken her healthy, strong father away from
her (and her family) for too long. He had come back a
changed man—a man in ill health who had lost too many
years to his captors. *Russians* had done this to her family
and her father! But if this deep-seated anger came to the
surface of her consciousness, she would quickly dismiss it.
As the years passed, Carmen's anger became nothing but a
faint shadow she pushed down and away. But, as she was
later to admit, God decided it was time Carmen dealt with
her long-buried resentment. What better way to bring her
to a point of confrontation than by sending her to the
people for whom she held so little regard? So, to Russia her
God called her and to Russia she and her husband went.

After only a few short months home in the U.S. to prepare for their midlife adventure, Carmen and Gunther
arrived on their newest mission field in January 1994. Her
first days in the chilly Russian winter brought one surprise
after another. Jesus began chipping away at Carmen's
secret wall of prejudice. As she disembarked from the

train on Russian soil for the first time, she thought, *There has been no change here in fifty years!* The Russians, not knowing this couple was more Indonesian than American in many ways, swarmed her and Gunther.

"We love Americans!" they proclaimed in their zeal.

Carmen met Christians who told them that, for years under Communism, they had met together secretly to praise and worship God. Because of the real threat of persecution and punishment, at their small gatherings the Christians would silently mouth hymns of praise together. That was how they "sang" their praises to God.

Babushkas, elderly Russian women, were everywhere. Throughout her time in Russia Carmen could not get over the clout—you might call it the raw power—that elderly Russian women command in their culture. We know of the past power of the KGB; we know of the horrible tales we now hear of the so-called "Russian Mafia." But none of them wields the power of one Russian Babushka who is crossed! These grandmothers and aunts of the Great Bear aren't easily intimidated, meek lambs when they hit their sixties and seventies. Their word is law. And heaven help the poor, hapless braggadocio who thinks otherwise!

One more thing Carmen and Gunther had to grow accustomed to in Russia was the "exuberant kissing and hugging going on among good friends and family." She wrote in a letter:

Gunther used to feel uncomfortable in Indonesia, walking down the street and having his hand held by another man. It was just a sign of friendship there. He is now learning to graciously accept and to even give loud, smacking, Christian-brotherly kisses, right on the mouth, as a special sign of friendship and acceptance. The first time it happened, it did take Gunther by surprise. It was a dear old man who just puckered up and pulled Gunther down [Gunther stands six-foot, four-inches tall] to plant that kiss on his lips.

In these small and large ways the Russian people won Carmen's heart. When she tells of her and Gunther's brief years in Russia, she says she can only echo C. S. Lewis's statement that she was "Surprised by Joy" to find herself so captivated by the people she had so long regarded with disdain. God had brought her full circle in her lifetime. Not only had He crushed her previous prejudice in the faces and hearts of a people she grew to love, He had "saved the best for last."

Carmen is now a retired missionary stateswoman encouraging others to heed God's commands. But she is also something else. Carmen—who at one time got angry when she was called "Russian," who, as a little girl, hated the Russians who had captured her earthly father —had one more surprise given her from the hand of her heavenly Father. She learned that she herself is intimately connected to the Russians she once regarded with such abject esteem. Carmen is a direct descendant of one of those power-wielding Russian matriarchs. She is the granddaughter of a Babushka!

CHAPTER 19
Her Colorful Life

Inez was born in Tennessee, but the lure of better-paying jobs and opportunities attracted her parents to move to the Great Lakes region of the United States in the 1920s. So move they did. They packed up bag and baggage and their three daughters and headed north. The three sisters were close. When Opal, the middle child, entered high school, she continued to take Inez, eight years her junior, with her everywhere. That included being taken along on some of Opal's dates, much to the chagrin of Opal's boyfriends. A date then was not what it is now. A short drive around the countryside for the pleasure of it or a brief trip to get ice cream was the sum total of most dates. But what a treat it was for "tagalong Inez," as one of Opal's boyfriends called her!

In her early school years Inez was introverted and aloof; that was just her nature. But her reserved demeanor was misinterpreted by her school chums as haughtiness. It was one of those "they thought that she thought that they thought she was too good for them" scenarios that left Inez troubled. She wanted to be liked and she wanted to have friends. So, she made a decision in sixth grade—a rather major decision for an eleven-year-old girl. She wouldn't be introverted anymore! She wouldn't be aloof! She would be extroverted and outgoing and just love people to pieces—demonstrably—and they would love her back! It wasn't long before Inez found herself surrounded by others who liked her and whom she in turn liked. Her carefully thoughtout and acted upon decision was a pivotal one. She was up and running in what would turn out to be a very colorful life!

Soon the Great Depression came along and Inez's father was out of work like millions of other Americans. Their family managed in those days like so many other American families managed following the stock market's blackest days. They got along by settling for second best. Inez and her mother would walk to the bakery near them to get day-old rolls. They didn't buy new shoes; Dad repaired the old ones. Their neighbor across the street owned a grocery store. He offered Inez's father odd jobs whenever he could. Inez's mother was delighted to receive old fruit from their neighbor that exceeded ripe. No problem there! She simply canned it! Inez's mother, a talented seamstress, made all her own and the girls' clothes. Inez's father became the family's beautician. He would cut the girls' hair when needed. It was the way life was and, in all the important ways, they were none the worse for it. The gray days of the Depression had many pinpoints of light and color.

As the 1930s continued their upward progression, Saturday nights were Grand Ole Opry nights. The family gathered around the radio and Inez's dad played the fiddle along with the music. Other nights the Young People's Group from their church gathered at their home. The growing teenagers would stand or sit around the piano to sing both hymns and popular music. Popcorn, cocoa, and cookies were their refreshments. As things slowly improved economically, ten cents not only provided admission to a movie, but sometimes a piece of dinnerware as well! So with God's provision in unique and simple ways, Inez's family of five weathered the lean years—with a kaleidoscope of love and laughter.

In high school the man who would eventually become her husband dated one of her best friends. Inez was the girl in the backseat then. She observed the back of Frank's head on all these excursions. As the Depression's grip on the American economy loosened, Inez and her friends were able to be out and about and enjoying fun things. But the pastel time between the world wars was waning.

Sometime after that guy in the front seat had dated not one, but *both* of Inez's best friends, he asked her out. It was years after they had finished high school. . .and just before December 7, 1941, became etched in the American consciousness for decades to come. Inez graduated to the front seat to sit next to the elusive Frank. Two years later the effervescent Inez assumed a permanent position next to Frank. She donned white and became his wife.

One of their most unique wedding gifts was a two-week stay in a cottage. This wasn't just any cottage! There was a button on the floor they only had to step on to summon the hired help. They had people to wait on their every beck and call! It was a dreamy, once in a lifetime, extravagant, castle-building-in-the-sand honeymoon they long cherished. . .except for the one night when the bed collapsed beneath them!

Frank was already a serviceman when they were married; army khaki was his color. Initially it wasn't too bad of an arrangement for the newlyweds. He was stationed close by and was able to come home on weekends. But a short stint in Europe ended his tour of duty at home. Inez found herself at home alone. She was not unlike a lot of women in their twenties then, and she and her girlfriends created opportunities to make the best of their shared separations.

In the months Frank was gone, Inez's "green" consisted of a staggering twelve dollars a week from her six days per week job. She and her friends would spend part of their hard-earned paychecks on a dinner and a black-and-white movie after work. Afterward they all boarded a bus or the streetcar (none of them had cars or the gasoline to put in them) for home. Sometimes they would have "sleepovers." They were single women and married women building friendships and supporting each other while their boyfriends and husbands were away at war.

By the fall of 1945 the black swastikas and red suns no longer colored the lives of people throughout the world. Fall became winter, but American servicemen were still scattered throughout the world, Frank included.

Inez's blue eyes take on a special sparkle as she recalls Christmas of that year.

"That was the most memorable Christmas of my life. I lived with my in-laws while Frank was stationed in Paris. The war was over, but Frank, like so many others, hadn't made it home yet. We were celebrating our Christmas without him when the doorbell rang. We went to the door and there he was! I couldn't believe it! He was home! Home for Christmas! He had been returned stateside. He immediately hopped on a train and traveled all night so he could be home for Christmas!" Her smile deepened as she recalled the holiday over fifty years in the past. "It was the best Christmas gift I ever received," she said reflectively.

Pink would be the dominant color of their lives for the next few years. Frank and Inez soon had two little girls to brighten their lives. Neither of their girls made her debut into the world without some anxious moments for both Inez and Frank. As labor began for their first daughter, it was clear they had better get to the hospital—sparkling white snow or no—and quickly!

Easier said than done.

Frank ran out to the car, slipped in the heaven-sent powder, and did a full-body, face-first plunge into a snowbank. They laughed about it years later. (But it wasn't all that funny the night it happened for the first-time father-to-be.) With daughter number two, Frank almost made it into the city newspaper under the headline: "Local Man Becomes Midwife on the Road." Inez wasn't at the hospital but ten minutes when her second daughter was born. It was something Inez would write about on the occasion of her and Frank's silver wedding anniversary. But at the time, neither she nor Frank was thinking in terms of "memorable event." Sheer *panic* drove the driver (whose face was doubtless drained of all color) that night!

For some years their lives progressed pleasantly and normally as Frank worked at his father's real estate company and Inez worked at home rearing their two girls. Then in 1957 Inez made another of those life-defining decisions as she had done in sixth grade.

The black-and-blue years of skinned-up knees that

her girls, like all children, had passed through had faded. Her daughters were becoming young ladies. They had traded in their occasional scrapes and bruises for the colors of cosmetics. Perhaps that's where Inez got her idea for a more colorful life.

"I loved being a wife and mother. But I was ready to tackle something new and totally different! I was looking for something more—and I found it!"

Inez took the proverbial plunge and auditioned for a part in a local theater production. She got the part! Inez was about to become an actress!

Her first part was a fun role. She donned flashy clothes, big jewelry, and heavy makeup. She flounced about the stage and the audience loved her. Frank and her daughters were her biggest fans, cheering her on from the first row. Inez's life became one of bright lights and vivid colors and she reveled in it.

" 'On with the show!' became a rallying cry for me!" she said with a laugh, pulling out well-worn scripts she has kept for over a quarter of a century. She looked through the stacks, remembering unique things about each role she played for over a decade.

In the play *Anastasia*, Inez played a charwoman. She spelled out the Russian phrases and words she had to use phonetically. It was the only way she could learn them! Her days in the theater gave her frustration, tension, and harried moments. But they also gave her exhilaration, fun, and challenge. She met and made new friends as well—people from all walks of life who, like her, wanted to try something completely new and different.

"Some of the people were like me, some were professionals. Some were out and out kooks, but we all had one thing in common," she said. "We loved this thing we call 'live production.' "

But it wasn't all up-front work. As a local theater troupe, everyone in the productions helped out in numerous ways. Not all of the "parts" were glamorous.

"We usually made our own costumes. We had to clean the theater. If we weren't in the show, we ushered, sold soda pop at the concession stand, and painted flats for scenery. That was colorful in another way!" she quips. "Nobody," she said with intensity, "got paid. Not even the director. But then, we weren't in it for the money!"

Inez even tried her hand at directing, but cameo parts remained her favorite. "There were fewer lines to learn, less pressure, and more fun!" she says in reflection. Through it all her family members were her most ardent supporters. Frank brought a bouquet of roses to each of her first-night performances and her girls always had plenty of eager, excited hugs for her afterward.

This time of Inez's life ended almost as abruptly as it had begun, however. And this time the change was forced upon her. At thirty-eight Inez had become a "blond bombshell" on the stage. But at fifty-one she had to leave it all behind. A heart attack made it too difficult for her to go on. For her, the spotlight had gone out. She returned to the life she had known before. Frank had stood by her through it all, good times and bad. Stellar performances and forgotten lines. . .long evenings painting scenery or sewing costumes. . .By now her daughters were grown and out of the house. So, it was simply Inez and Frank again, just as it had been since the days of the honeymoon cottage. Fortunately, the colorless days immediately following her heart attack in 1971 did not continue forever. Ever so gradually, Inez's life took on a rosy hue once again.

If you meet Inez today, you are likely to see her "dressed to the nines," as they say, at church. Or, she might be helping out her sister, Opal, who now takes her turn and "tags along" with Inez. Inez is still as outgoing and extroverted as she was circa 1930. She glowingly greets friends and acquaintances with a warm enthusiasm and zeal that's rare in many people who are eighty. Ever since her first life-changing decision as a young girl, she's been, as she puts it, "huggin' and kissin' everybody." And she does! She positively glows with affection and *joie de vivre*, as the French say. She is not acting—that's just her! She is a fun-loving, vibrant lady, even though she had to set aside her midlife love affair with acting.

"I simply had too much difficulty trying to memorize

lines after my heart attack," Inez says now with a light shrug of her shoulders. "It was great fun while it lasted! And, oh, how I enjoyed it!"

Inez may be in what many people call her "sunset years," but for her that term doesn't mean she's slowing down or sitting around. She is as vibrant as the array of beautiful sunsets that conclude her busy days! Her life on the stage was colorful, but perhaps not quite as colorful as her real life, painted by the Master Artist Himself.

CHAPTER 20
A Story Behind the Story

The year was 1971. Al, a grade school principal, sat with three university students in his office. Under a grant awarded by the federal government called the Teacher Corps, these young people were going to be teachers—a new breed of teachers. They were college dropouts, disgruntled with education. Yet here they were, aspiring to be educators. Convinced they could be and would be better educators than the present folk who were in the teaching profession, they had a set of ideas about what was right and wrong in the classroom. Not the least of which was the classroom setting itself. They were going to change that. They had an agenda.

One young man in particular had "challenge" etched in every feature of his face. His attire, his attitude, and his body language reinforced the message that needed few, if any, words to be readily apparent. He didn't like the way things were, and he was going to change them: for the students they were going to teach, for those with whom they would be working, for the society in which he lived. That this young man and his colleagues were radicals in every sense of the word was clear to the pensive man sitting behind the desk. The challenger was barely able to conceal his angry, confrontational demeanor under the cloak of his best interview conduct.

Al, the principal sitting behind the desk, had spent a lifetime giving careful respect to others and patiently letting them have their say. This young gentleman had not learned such personal qualities as yet. Al listened as the self-appointed spokesman told him their ideas. But one thought kept nagging at Al as he listened. *This is the kind of kid who would just as soon shoot me the minute I turned my back.*

"The first thing we need to do is get rid of the American flag in the classrooms," the challenger said, continuing his vindictive monologue on educational change. "I hate that flag. It shouldn't be there."

Al nodded his head thoughtfully as he looked at this blond, middle-class young man who had grown up in a rural setting—just as Al himself had. Al suspected that was where the similarities between the two of them began. And ended. He took advantage of a brief pause in the intern's harangue.

"Was there a flag in your classroom in school when you were growing up?" he asked quietly.

"Yes, there was." Belligerent. Defiant. Challenging. Three words spoken, three words unspoken.

"Is that when you decided it shouldn't be in the classroom?" Al inquired further.

"No, I just know it now," the intern returned, his reply curtly polite.

"Then you weren't forced to think one way or the other about it back then?" Al asked. "You were given the opportunity to think about it for yourself?"

"Well, yes," the college dropout said, somewhat more subdued now, not sure what Al's point was.

"We need to give these kids the same opportunity you had." Al met the hard eyes and tight mouth of the challenger with steady intensity. "It's our business," he said evenly and kindly, "to teach children how to think. Not what to think."

In the months immediately following this interview, Al did not change what he had done as a teacher and continued to do as an elementary school principal. He went to the homes of the students. He went to the homes of many who did not have the same advantages the young challenger had had growing up. Al took the challenger with him on a number of these visits. Often the homes of the children Al visited were neither stable nor lovingly functional. Many of the students grew up in what is euphemistically called "The Projects." Al would walk up to the door, introduce himself, and then pop his primary question to the child's parents or guardian: "What can I do to help your child learn?"

He always listened courteously, respectfully to the answer. It was a habit of his life. Then he would make his contribution or suggestion as to how the parent or parents could help him help their growing child. In this way, they would be a team, working together toward the same goal. They would be partners in helping the child get the best out of his or her education.

These visits were an eye-opening experience for Al's teaching interns, who had never been in the Projects before—especially for the radical university dropout who was out to change the world. For Al it was a simple but time-demanding, commitment-oriented way to do the best he could do educationally for his students. He did not do it for the interns' benefit; he simply allowed them to go along with him and observe what he had found worked for him and his students through the years.

Were the rewards showstoppers? Did his grassroots attempts to connect with the families of the children in his school make headlines? Of course not. The reward was in the details, which Al never missed.

"Last night we all made supper together!" said one little girl once, her eyes dancing with the new experience.

"I got to play with my dad!" announced a little boy to Al soon after Al made the acquaintance of his father. Apparently, that man decided if Al could take such an active interest in his son, so could he. This personal touch made Al very approachable as far as the students were concerned, too. One day a little first grader came up to him. She smiled and gazed up at him with open delight. "That is a beautiful jacket!" she said to her school principal, her eyes full of sparkling admiration.

"Why, thank you!" Al replied. It was new, after all! How sweet of this young child to notice!

"It looks just like a pajama top!" she declared in her innocence, continuing on her way.

Al's contact with children and their families showed the Rebel with a Cause that genuine interest in people as people could be a far more compelling—and just as radical—method of making his world a better place. More so than ditching the American flag or getting out of the traditional classroom setting. Long before these interns came, and long after they left, it was the way Al did things during his thirty-plus years in education.

Funny thing is, Al had never planned to be an educator. He had planned to be, and had been educated to be, an electrical engineer. As sometimes happens, however, God had other plans for Al. Just how God took Al from an interest in electrical engineering to teaching little children is a story in itself. That story really begins with Al's father, Charles.

Although Al grew up in a rural setting just as his defiant teaching intern had, there was nothing else similar in their backgrounds. Al grew up in rural, southern Alabama where the community population topped out at twenty-nine. "Including the livestock and the nine of us," he adds with a chuckle. Not unlike most of the U.S. back in the 1920s, large families and small communities like Al's were the order of the day. Powerful combines with headlights hadn't yet supplanted the predominantly manual labor of farmers and sharecroppers who worked hard for their living from sunup until sundown. Automation did not yet dominate farming.

Clara, Al's grandmother, worked diligently for her little house and three acres of land. She washed and ironed clothes for another large family every week for nine months. She was paid three dollars a month for her labor and with the money she paid her annual note of twenty-seven dollars. The three dollars a month she made ironing was three dollars more a month than she had made at her previous career. Clara had been a black slave in her first sixteen years of life. She had learned hard work under great duress and with no choice in the matter.

When Clara was thirteen years old, she was torn

away from her family. She was given as a wedding gift from her owner to his daughter. She would be the new bride's maid as the young white woman began her life far from her father's plantation and in her own home. Not until seventy years later would Clara ever see another member of her family again. But with the end of the Civil War came the end of Clara's slavery. She began working for what she, for the first time in her life, could own.

As the years quickly passed and she became an independent, working woman, Clara's family grew. Clara had eleven children, one of whom was Charles, Al's father. Like a number of his sisters, Charles was mulatto. One day, Charles's mixed blood would work for the deliverance of one of his own sons. That day, however, was still in the distant future. For now, young Charles had his own life to carve out while growing up in the Deep South during the last years of the nineteenth century.

Three months out of the year he went to school in a one-room log cabin. On Mondays he would fetch the clothes from several white families. His mother continued the washing and ironing of laundry to support her family. On Fridays he would return the laundered and ironed items. Between those two days he went to his small school where he learned to read and write.

When he was ten, Charles began plowing their farm.

He and his sisters who were still at home helped his mother with farming and odd jobs in the community for their daily living. At fourteen Charles began working in a logging camp, where he learned how to cook for large groups of loggers. His work there not only netted him extra money in tips (his cooking was considered the best by the loggers), it also gave him opportunity to save and marry his childhood sweetheart, Harriett, several years later.

Charles and his wife began homesteading in 1912 in the same small community where Charles grew up. They started their own family and Charles set about becoming an influential man in his community, segregated as it was from its white counterpart. He owned a lot of land and employed many people to harvest his cotton crop. His own children helped as well on the farm as they grew older. During bad crop years, Charles would return to the logging camp in order to meet the mortgage payment on his home. He learned machining and became a blacksmith, too. This made him a valuable resource to his fellow farmers and was another way to support his growing family.

Charles worked even harder, if possible, than his mother. He was part farmer, part merchant, and part landlord. He was an imaginative entrepreneur, trying his hand at a variety of vocations and succeeding at most, if not all, of them.

When Al was born, his daddy, Charles, made sure he and all Al's siblings became hard workers as well—from the time they were small. They started out working hard in school, as well as on the farm. Because of the planting and harvesting cycle, school was in session from October to early April.

There was nothing easy about growing up black in the Deep South during the first half of the 1900s. Al's education, like that of his siblings, was a "one-book education." All the schools in the South were still segregated when Al grew up, so the black children were limited to one book for social studies, one book for math, and one book for reading. Their three-room schoolhouse was small and had no reference books or library.

African-Americans were not allowed in the (white) libraries. So, the math book, the reader, and any other available textbooks remained at the school. Year after year after year.

"That's the way it was," Al says with a shrug of his shoulders.

When Al was eight years old, his mother died suddenly after a brief illness. There was a bumper crop harvest that year, Al recalls, making their work alongside their father even more difficult without the wise and womanly touch of his mother.

Charles remarried a few years later. But work continued to dictate many of their days. Now the older children were old enough to start attending high school and soon college. The work ethic that was such a part of Al's father's constitution was continually being reinforced by the growing needs of his family. He worked hard; his kids worked hard. It was a fact of their daily lives.

Another fact of life where Al grew up was the Ku Klux Klan. As a little boy, Al grew up in the middle of Klandom. Sharecroppers, like his father, were expected to attend what were, without apology, called "lynchings." The Klan and the sheriff were all essentially one and the same. There was no help from the law for the black man when the Klan was involved—or any other time, quite honestly. Although Al himself, as a child, was not required to attend these gruesome events, another too-frequent occurrence remains in his store of memories: Klan rallies.

One of Al's vivid childhood memories was the night he was almost abducted by the Klan. Somehow Al ended up at the wrong place at the wrong time. He was simply walking alongside the road, minding his own business. One minute he was safe, the next he was in the middle of a hate-charged crowd! The Klan members came from everywhere and nowhere all at once!

A son of Al's white grandfather was among them. The Klan members did not know this man was Al's uncle, but Al knew. And Al's white uncle knew. Seeing what was about to happen, Al's uncle gave him a rough shove to the ground, making it look like a well-aimed punch. Al played his part well in the terrifying minutes of the torch-lit night. He stumbled backward, falling to the ground farther from the torches and center of the hate-charged maelstrom.

"This one's mine!" his uncle announced in an angry voice. No one contested his assertive declaration. It was only one black child. The God these men claimed to serve blinded their vision. As their attention turned elsewhere, Al's uncle turned back to him, loudly whispering a solitary word for his ears alone.

"RUN!"

Al ran.

He ran until he was out of harm's way. The moment of terror had passed. Narrowly. The white hoods and torches went noisily in another direction. Al's uncle faded into the cover of night, making sure Al got a safe distance from the mob. Al, gasping for breath, ran to the safety of his home. He was safe! It was a terrifying experience he has never forgotten.

Not all of Al's life growing up was hard work or isolated nights of terror. The sense of community ran strong among Al's family and other sharecroppers. Like most southern black families, Al's family's social life centered in the church. The gatherings were small, but always well attended. Since their church only had services once a month, however, the family went to a different church every week. For Al this wasn't all bad.

"Church was the place where one met girls!" he says, laughing. It was also where Al met Jesus. Al's Savior and Lord would mold him as a man who would live with determination, laughter, and affirmation. Al would not become a man crippled by a festering, bitter anger, as easy as it would have, or could have, been for him.

As a teenager, Al left home to attend Tuskegee Institute, where he completed his high school education and began working on his college degree in electrical engineering. Students of Tuskegee had a vested interest in their school. Many, like Al, helped pay their tuition by building dormitories at the school.

Because he was in the Reserve Officers Training Corps, Al was given an unforgettable assignment as a student. In late 1942, one of America's most well known botanists and chemists died. Because of the high regard in which this pioneer was held by the staff and students at Tuskegee and in the community, the funeral service was not scheduled to take place until all the students had returned from the Christmas/New Year's break. Al was one who kept vigil at the casket until the day of the funeral. The man who had died would long be remembered in American history. He was given a fitting service of remembrance. The man's name was George Washington Carver.

Like other young men during the mid-1940s, Al's college education was interrupted by Uncle Sam. Soon after being drafted, Al found himself on a troop transport ship, ready to leave San Diego for the war in the Pacific theater. Al, optimistic about one day returning to Tuskegee and picking up where he left off, watched the California coastline as his ship began its journey out to sea. He wasn't depressed about going off to war; it was something he had to do, just like so many others. He found himself standing at the rail of the ship next to a sobbing, waving sailor. He didn't have to ask his teary shipmate what was troubling him. The man told him without inquiry.

"I know I'm never gonna see my wife again!" the sailor blubbered. "I just know I'll never come back from this war!"

Al didn't want to seem unsympathetic, but he had other plans once the war ended. And he wasn't about to dwell on any other possibility. He pulled out a pencil and paper.

"Give me your address," he said good-naturedly. "I'm plannin' on coming back and I'll check on her for you!"

Al served on Guam for the next two years of World War II. He was attached to the Seabees for a period of time and served as a naval electrician. "There wasn't one building on the island that didn't have a hole in it," he says with the remembering.

There wasn't much electrical line that survived the frequent bombing raids either. Al spent his time in Guam putting up much-needed communication and electrical lines for the American forces in the Pacific. Over and over and over again. He also spent a lot of time loading ships for attacks on other islands in the Pacific. It was grueling work in the intense sunshine and heat. The war on Guam was unlike that in Europe. When they weren't contending with firepower from ships or aircraft, guerrilla warfare was the order of the day.

"You got worried," Al says, "when the constant shooting stopped."

After the war ended, Al served as a maintenance supervisor for the base. But when he came home from the service, things had changed little in Alabama. He had served his country as had hundreds of thousands of others, but he was still a black man living in the Deep South. His uniform made little difference.

"If white men or women came walking down the sidewalk, I still had to get off it until they passed. That's just the way it was."

Al joined the Air Force ROTC after World War II and became a second lieutenant. This earned him a short stint in the Korean conflict. His focus remained on completing his college education, however, and earning his degree in electrical engineering. But once Al completed his college education, there were no jobs to be had in his home state for a black electrical engineer. Not even at the power company where Al had worked while a student (at student wages) as boss of a line crew. No one was interested in his experience or credentials. Al turned to another profession as a result: teaching.

First Al taught black veterans. Then he went on to teach in schools. Sitting in a meeting for new teachers in his district, he met the woman who would be his wife. They had their first date on Halloween. As a chaperon at a school party, the chaperon (Al) took his own date. Three short months later he and Juanita were married.

Al and his wife spent three more years in Alabama. For a short time he and Juanita attended Dexter Avenue Baptist Church, where Dr. Martin Luther King Jr. was pastor.

"Martin," Al says with intensity, "could motivate people with a word. He needed no strongman tactics." He hesitates as he remembers this unique man of God and agent of social change. "He could motivate people to put themselves in harm's way for what they believed," he says.

Dr. King and others were catalysts of change. Al knows; he was there. He marched in protest of, prayed about, and challenged the double standards of American culture with Dr. King and others. It was the beginning of some better things, not the least of which was equal education for all American children. The days were coming to an end when black children had a single, decades-old book from which to learn about history or science.

In the course of these later, transitional years, Al and his family eventually came to Ohio. It was there that he met the radical college dropout who was out to change the world. Al's challenge to the challenger was that the young man get to know his young charges, as well as teach them. That teaching intern never knew one iota about Al's life growing up. This young man came to Al hateful and angry. But Al had never been taught hate.

"In all the years I sat at my grandmother's knee," Al says, "I never heard her speak a bitter word about anyone. Anyone. Anytime." It was the same with his father. But Al did not need to teach the intern his own learned lessons by word. He instructed him by example. He let the children themselves be the would-be educator's real teachers.

"The kids changed him. They changed them all," Al says reflectively. "The kids loved them—they loved him —and they showed it." The young adults of the Teaching Corps learned their lessons well in the "traditional classrooms" that were really not so traditional after all.

There are a few more things you might want to know about the three men of this tale: Al's father, Charles; the renegade student intern Al mentored in his elementary school; and Al himself, as he has now joined the ranks of the retired.

Charles did not retire until he was ninety-five—and only then because he gave a customer a quarter in change for a nickel. He figured it was time to retire if he couldn't make the right change! He had outlived his first wife, Harriett, his second wife, Essie, and finally his dear wife of thirty years, Lillian. When Lillian died, Charles's desire to carry on died as well. He passed away two months later. He had lived on this earth for 104 years before he went on to bigger enterprises at the side of his heavenly Father.

The rebellious student intern, who so resented authority and hated the American flag, went on to serve under it (and authority) in the military. He called Al some years after his internship to thank him for the lessons he learned as his junior colleague. He humbly asked Al for a written recommendation—for a teaching position. Al wrote him one. The radical, former student had obviously done some learning and growing.

Al is now seventy-five and going strong. He's been known to go play golf after his chemo treatments. He is a deacon in his church and runs up the steps to the altar to talk about the Lord's faithfulness in his life. When he shares moments of his "rich, wonderful" (his words) and fascinating life with others, he doesn't speak of his bouts with colon, liver, and lung cancer over the last several years. In fact, he hardly mentions them at all.

"I'm at peace with this cancer," he says with a wave of his hand. "The Lord's got everything under control. He's got something here for me to do. I just hope I recognize it when it comes along."

Something tells me he will.

Katherine Anne Douglas started writing stories almost as soon as she could hold one of those fat, first grade pencils. Fascinated with people's lives, she's written a number of stories and articles (both fiction and nonfiction), many of which have been published in a variety of journals and magazines. *Short Stories from Days Gone By* is her third published book. Kathy and her husband, Mark, live in the farming community of Berkey, Ohio.